"Is it acceptable to have sex before one is...um...married?" Janella asked.

Thomas felt his eyebrows shoot up. "You cut right to the chase, don't you?" If his hands were unsteady, it was just because he hadn't had a cup of coffee yet this morning. And he could—and would—answer what was a perfectly logical question in a calm and professional manner.

"That's kind of complicated. I guess these days it's pretty much a matter of personal choice. Some people consider it immoral, some don't."

"And what is your personal choice?"

"That's a personal question, Janella. You can't just go around asking people about their sex lives."

"I'm not asking just anyone. I'm asking you."

D0950546

Dear Reader,

We've got one of our most irresistible lineups ever for you this month, and you'll know why as soon as I start talking about the very first book. With *The Return of Rafe MacKade*, *New York Times* bestseller Nora Roberts begins a new miniseries, The MacKade Brothers, that will move back and forth between Intimate Moments and Special Edition. Rafe is also our Heartbreaker for the month, so don't get your heart broken by missing this very special book!

Romantic Traditions continues with Patricia Coughlin's *Love in the First Degree*, a compelling spin on the "wrongly convicted" story line. For fans of our Spellbound titles, there's *Out-Of-This-World Marriage* by Maggie Shayne, a marriage-of-convenience story with a star-crossed—and I mean that literally!— twist. Finish the month with new titles from popular authors Terese Ramin with *A Certain Slant of Light*, Alexandra Sellers with *Dearest Enemy*, as well as *An Innocent Man* by an exciting new writer, Margaret Watson.

This month, and every month, when you're looking for exciting romantic reading, come to Silhouette Intimate Moments—and enjoy!

Yours,

Leslie J. Wainger
Senior Editor and Editorial Coordinator

Please address questions and book requests to:
Silhouette Reader Service
U.S.: 3010 Walden Ave., P.O. Box 1325, Buffalo, NY 14269
Canadian: P.O. Box 609, Fort Erie, Ont. L2A 5X3

OUT-OF-THIS-WORLD MARRIAGE

MAGGIE SHAYNE

Published by Silhouette Books

America's Publisher of Contemporary Romance

If you purchased this book without a cover you should be aware
that this book is stolen property. It was reported as "unsold and
destroyed" to the publisher, and neither the author nor the
publisher has received any payment for this "stripped book."

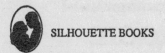 SILHOUETTE BOOKS

ISBN 0-373-07633-9

OUT-OF-THIS-WORLD MARRIAGE

Copyright © 1995 by Margaret Benson

All rights reserved. Except for use in any review, the reproduction
or utilization of this work in whole or in part in any form by any
electronic, mechanical or other means, now known or hereafter
invented, including xerography, photocopying and recording, or in
any information storage or retrieval system, is forbidden without
the written permission of the editorial office, Silhouette Books,
300 East 42nd Street, New York, NY 10017 U.S.A.

All characters in this book have no existence outside the imagination of
the author and have no relation whatsoever to anyone bearing the same
name or names. They are not even distantly inspired by any individual
known or unknown to the author, and all incidents are pure invention.

This edition published by arrangement with Harlequin Enterprises B.V.

® and TM are trademarks of Harlequin Enterprises B.V., used under
license. Trademarks indicated with ® are registered in the United States
Patent and Trademark Office, the Canadian Trade Marks Office and in
other countries.

Printed in U.S.A.

Books by Maggie Shayne

Silhouette Intimate Moments

Reckless Angel #522
Miranda's Viking #568
Forgotten Vows...? #598
Out-Of-This-World Marriage #633

Silhouette Shadows

* *Twilight Phantasies* #18
* *Twilight Memories* #30
Kiss of the Shadow Man #38
**Twilight Illusions* #47

*Wings in the Night

MAGGIE SHAYNE

lives in a rural community in central New York with her husband and five daughters. She's currently serving as president of the Central New York chapter of the Romance Writers of America and has been invited to join the National League of American Pen Women. In her spare time, Maggie enjoys speaking about writing at local schools and conducting a romance-writing workshop at a local community college. Her debut novel, *Reckless Angel,* was a finalist for the RITA Award for Best First Book of 1994.

To Stacie,
for being sweet and wonderful,
and for saying at least six times a day,
"I love you, Mommy."
I love you, too, sweetheart.

Prologue

Thomas always knew when they would come. He didn't know *how* he knew. He just did. It was like some buzzing kind of feeling inside his head. He'd wake from a sound sleep, knowing they were there. He was never afraid of them. And he never told anyone. He was certain that no one would believe him anyway, and doubly certain that if he did say anything he'd be sure to get a long lecture on his overactive imagination and the difference between lies and make-believe from his dad. Dad hated lies. He didn't want to tell his dad anything that might even sound like a lie. But there was something else, too. Something inside him that made him keep quiet. He thought maybe they didn't want him to tell. So he didn't.

They were his own special secret. And on dark summer nights, when that buzzing sensation rang in his ears, Thomas would get out of bed and climb through the window and down the trellis in his pajamas. He'd run as fast as he could, around back through the tall, damp grass in his bare feet. Past the barn and through the wheat fields and up the little hill near the stream beyond them. And he'd sit there with the wind blowing his hair and the wheat dancing in the breeze and the stars twinkling overhead. And he'd watch them pass, blazing greenish lights in the sky, igniting the whole world for just a second. He'd wave his hands, always having the odd feeling that they knew. That they could see him there. That someone was waving back at him. And he'd go back to bed feeling good.

But this night was different. Tonight there was something else ringing in his ears, and the buzzing was louder, deeper. More urgent. The sounds beyond the buzzing worried him. They sounded like crying. Someone small and frightened, crying. He puzzled over that for a second or two. It wasn't like he could really *hear* it. More like he *felt* it. Soft sobs tearing at his chest, only they weren't his.

He had the oddest feeling that something was wrong.

Thomas pulled open the drawer of the desk beside his bed and took out his slingshot. He stroked the smooth, gleaming handle where he'd carved his initials. He'd better take it along, just in case.

When he pushed open the window cool air rushed in to chill him, so he grabbed his jacket off the bedpost and slipped it on, dropping the slingshot in the pocket. Then he climbed out the window, down the trellis just like always, and he started off over the back lawn and through the wheat fields. He ran a little faster than usual. That sense that something was wrong got stronger the farther he went.

For some reason, he didn't stop at the little knoll near the stream tonight. Something told him that wasn't far enough. Whatever was wrong wasn't here. It was in the woods just beyond.

He muttered his only cuss word, wishing he'd for once remembered his dad's reminders to wear shoes when he went outside. The ground was cold, and in the woods it was rough and uneven, with gnarled roots reaching up to trip him. Too late to go back for shoes now, though. He didn't know where he was going. He didn't know why; he just knew he had to, so he went.

The woods grew thicker. He shouldn't feel nervous. He played here all the time. But it sure was different at night, darker, of course, and so quiet. Usually there were birds making so much racket you could barely hear yourself think. Not tonight, though. Even the wind seemed to have decided not to come into these woods tonight. He shrugged a little deeper into his jacket. At least it was warmer here in the trees without that chilly wind.

And there was a *little* light. Moonlight, but it only came through the thick branches here and there, and it wasn't much help. It made odd, out-of-shape shadows that tried to scare him. Like that one just now. Looked just like a man walking, just beyond a stand of berry briars. But that was stupid. It was gone a second later. Just a shadow, that's all it was.

But now he saw an eerie green glow spilling into the woods. Seemed to be coming from the clearing right near the center, an open, grassy spot where he liked to go. He called it the secret meadow because it was so well hidden by the trees all around it. Thomas moved a little closer, trying to be as quiet as he could, though he didn't really know why he ought to.

Then he caught his breath and tried to stop his heart from hammering as he ducked behind a tree. Something very big and very bright sat in the secret meadow. It resembled a fat, green, glowing spider. He thought he knew what it was, but he didn't really want to know. He didn't even want to stay here and watch it, but he couldn't seem to look away.

Then that crying sound in his head got louder, and he turned. It was like some kind of superpowered magnet was pulling at him. But it was no magnet. It was that crying that drew him onward, deeper into the trees, farther than he'd ever been from his farm before.

He walked for quite a ways. He ought to be worried about getting lost out here, since he wasn't real familiar with this part of the woods. But he wasn't. The farther he went, the quicker he walked, and the crying sounds in his head got louder and louder.

And then they got all soft again. Only they were not in his head anymore. They were real, and he was hearing them with his ears. He followed the sounds and only muttered "Holy cow" when he finally found where they were coming from.

She sat huddled against a big oak tree with her knees drawn to her chest and a mass of black hair hiding her face. There was a pool of moonlight shining down on the spot where she sat, like some spotlight pointing her out to him. The poor little thing must be terrified out here all alone. She was shaking all over, and sobbing so hard it made his throat kind of swell up just to hear her. He started toward her, then froze in his tracks when he heard the growl from just beyond her.

He spotted the dog. She must have heard it, too, 'cause her head came up fast, eyes huge and scared looking, and she uttered a little shriek when she turned to see it behind her. The dog looked like a stray, skinny and mean, crouched and snarling a few feet from her.

Thomas's young shoulders straightened a little and he felt a rush of anger as he bent to scoop up a stone with one hand, yanking out his slingshot with the other. He took careful aim and let fly.

The stone pinged off the dog's head. It turned its ugly gaze on him, teeth bared. Thomas grabbed another rock, a bigger one, and this time he pegged the animal right on the snout. The dog gave a soft yelp.

"Go on, get out of here!" Thomas fitted another rock into the sling, but the dog was already turning tail and loping off when he released it.

Thomas smiled and looked at the girl. She stared back at him, wide-eyed, still afraid. He had to blink twice when he got a good look at her. She was the prettiest girl he'd ever seen, even in the pale moonlight. He figured she was about his age, maybe nine or ten. And without even asking her, he knew she was lost. He held out his hand. She only stared at it and bit her lip.

"It's okay," he told her. He wiggled his hand at her. "Really, it's okay. That dog won't come back."

She blinked, but didn't move. Maybe she didn't understand. He moved closer and bent a little, clasping her hand with his. He gave a gentle tug and she got to her feet, staring at the ground and brushing the leaves from her funny clothes with her free hand. Looked like a pair of coveralls, only they were black, and tight fitting, and he couldn't see a button or a zipper anywhere.

The small hand he held was cold and still shaking. He'd never seen anyone so scared before. He squeezed it a little and smiled at her so she'd know he was only trying to help. "I'm Thomas," he said softly. She frowned and tilted her head. "Thomas," he repeated. He dropped the slingshot into his pocket and pointed to his chest with his free hand when he said it this time.

Her lips moved a little. Not a smile, but almost. "Thom—us."

"Yeah, that's right. Thomas."

She dipped her head. Pointing to herself as he'd done, she said softly, "Janella."

"Janella." He nodded. "That's a real pretty name, Janella." He stared at her for a moment, amazed by her eyes. They were slanted a little and dark around the edges as if she were wearing makeup, only he knew she wasn't. With her dark hair and huge dark eyes she reminded him of some exotic princess. He shrugged out of his jacket, releasing her hand to do it. Then he settled it around her shoulders. Dad would be pleased with his good manners.

"Come on, Janella. Come with me." He started forward, and she snatched his hand again, holding on tight. She came with him, but he knew she was uncertain and still scared. "It's okay. Come on."

He kept talking to her that way, urging her along through the woods back the way he'd come. She clung to his hand the whole time. He'd never really thought it was much of a thrill to hold a girl's hand before, but he held hers anyhow. She was scared, and if it made her feel better, then he figured it was worth it. Besides, she was holding on so tight, he didn't think he could pull his away if he'd wanted to.

He walked slowly, so she could keep up, and it took quite a while to get back to the clearing. But as soon as that green glow spilled onto them, he knew he'd done the right thing. Her eyes got even bigger, and she smiled fully for the first time. He stood still for a second. Gosh, she was even prettier in the bright light. And before he knew what she was thinking, she threw her arms around his neck and hugged him so hard he could barely breathe.

When she released him, he looked at the ground, embarrassed. She took something from around her neck and put it around his. A charm of some sort, hanging from a light chain. Well, if that didn't beat everything. All he'd done was show her the way back. His spine got a little straighter, and for the first time in his life, Thomas Duffy felt like a real live hero.

She handed him his jacket, even as he was racking his brain to think of something to give her in return. He ought to give her *something*, hadn't he? He pulled his jacket on and stuffed his hands into the pockets. He'd forgotten all about the cold until now. The smooth wood of his slingshot touched his palm, and he nodded, pulling it out. It would make a good present. He'd carved it himself from an old beech tree, and he'd coated it in pretty brown stain and polyurethane so it gleamed. He'd worked for weeks on it. If anyone had told him a week ago that he'd willingly give it away to some strange, pretty girl, he'd have said they were nuts. But for some reason, he didn't mind parting with it now. He pressed it into her hand.

She looked at it, tilting her head one way and another. Then her head came up, as if she'd heard something, though Thomas hadn't heard a sound. She looked into his eyes once more, smiled gently at him, and for the first time in history, Thomas wondered what it would be like to kiss a girl. Really weird, since he didn't even like girls.

So why was his mind stuck on Janella's lips like this? He frowned a little, working up his nerve. But she turned and ran away, down into the clearing, disappearing into that blinding green light.

Thomas sighed long and hard. He ought to get home. But instead, he sat down on the cool, hard ground, and he waited.

A few seconds passed. No more. Then the light rose without a single sound. It flashed brighter, so bright he had to cover his eyes, and then it was gone.

Thomas sat there for a long time before he finally made himself get up and start back home. He felt good, really good. He'd done a good thing tonight, and he figured that if his dad knew about it, he'd be darned proud.

But his dad couldn't know. No one could. Thomas knew he had to keep the secret, the same way he'd known he had to come out here tonight. He vowed he'd do just that, even if it killed him. Besides, who'd believe him anyway?

The next morning, Dad showed him the article on the front page of the *Sumac Daily Star.* UFO Seen By Over 100! Dad said it was the silliest thing he'd ever heard. Thomas didn't say a word. Even when a carload of strangers in dark suits came around town asking questions about it, Thomas stuck to his promise.

For months and months after that strange night, he went out to the knoll and watched and waited, but he never saw them again. He never heard that buzzing sound that told him they were near. And he never saw that beautiful princess, except once or twice in his dreams.

Chapter 1

"Dr. Duffy!" The shout was accompanied by the front door of the big farmhouse slamming open. Thomas stopped with a forkful of Eugenia Overton's tuna casserole halfway to his mouth to glance up at the disheveled boy in the doorway. Grimacing, he dropped the fork and stood up. Damn women had a knack for going into labor just as he sat down to eat. It had happened every time on Karicau, that war-ravaged Third World island in the South Pacific where he'd spent the past eight years of his life. Thomas didn't know why he'd expected it to be any different here. Matthew Connor's pretty young mother wasn't going to be an exception. Except that she was strong and healthy, hadn't been suffering malnutrition through the entire pregnancy. And Thomas wouldn't have to dodge snipers' bullets in order to get to her.

Thomas reached to the shelf beside the front door for his bag and glanced back down at Matt. "So how far apart are they?"

The twelve-year-old only shook his head, his jaw working soundlessly, his pupils too dilated.

A skittery feeling crawled over Thomas's spine. Humphrey sensed it, too. The shaggy border collie had come from his customary spot under the table to stand beside Thomas, his ears pricked, the hair on his back bristling.

Gripping a skinny shoulder and giving it a firm shake, Thomas prodded the boy. "Snap out of it, Matthew. What's happened?"

The boy blinked, cornflower-blue eyes finally focusing on Thomas. "It's Dad...the tractor flipped...he's pinned, Doc. You gotta hurry."

Thomas felt the kid's hand gripping his arm, saw the desperation in the young eyes, and blocked both from his mind before there was time for a single emotion to surface there. An iron wall descended between him and this boy. It had to. This was a job. He was a doctor. He'd do what he could do, and that was that. If he'd learned anything on Karicau, that was it. You either kept your distance or lost your mind.

Matt was already running back down the driveway with Thomas on his heels. Hurrying because it was part of the job, not because he felt fear or worry. He didn't *feel* anything. Nothing at all.

The boy veered toward the battered pickup he'd left running. Thomas's hand closed on his shoulder, stopping him. "My Jeep, Matt." No twelve-year-old ought to be driving at all, let alone in the state Matthew was in now. "We'll get the pickup later."

Matt didn't argue. He ran to shut the truck off and was beside Thomas in the Jeep in a flash. Then they were bounding over the rutted Iowa roads, turning off into a partially harvested wheat field.

It was minutes, but it seemed longer. It always seemed longer. Thomas crouched beside Hugh Connor, felt his thready pulse, knew his chest was crushed. Damn fool man was pushing sixty. Had no business being on a tractor in the first place.

The neighbors had gathered, but Thomas closed his mind to their concerned murmuring until it was only a soft, distant drone. It was a little harder not to hear Shelly's quiet crying. She was too close, kneeling right beside Thomas, one arm protectively wrapped around her ballooning belly, the other, clutching Hugh's limp hand. She spoke to the husband who was nearly twice her age, though he couldn't hear her. "Thomas is here now, hon. He'll get you through this—you know he will. You'll be okay now. Thomas will take care—"

"Back off a little, Shelly."

She looked up, blinking at him, sky-blue eyes shimmering under a layer of tears, maybe a little startled at his tone of voice. But she nodded and shuffled backward. Then she reached out, touched Thomas's hand. "Don't you let him die, Thomas Duffy. Don't let him go."

He closed his eyes and tried to blot the plea from his memory. Filed it away with the thousands of others he'd heard, the wails of the mothers and wives, the cries of the children, the agonized screams of the wounded and the dying.

There wasn't time to wait for the volunteer fire department to arrive with the equipment that would make this safe. He'd already called for a chopper from the Jeep. ETA was ten minutes. The rest was up to him. Two other tractors backed up to the far side of the toppled machine. Men attached sturdy chains. They all knew what needed doing without being told. It wasn't the first time something like this had happened in Sumac. Farming was a treacherous profession. But at least everyone here had plenty to eat. There'd be no complications brought on by malnutrition and disease, and no danger of tripping a land mine if he put a foot down in the wrong spot. Hell, this was a breeze compared with where he'd spent most of the past decade.

Other men took their places, ready to brace the tractor to keep it from falling back onto Hugh once it was lifted. Thomas took the backboard from the Jeep's rear seat and returned to his position beside Hugh. Reluctantly, he inclined his head at Shelly, now standing with both arms around the son who looked more like her younger brother.

"Get over here, you two. Shelly, I need you to hold his head, just like this. Matthew, help her. Put your hands here and here. Don't let his neck twist at all. Okay?" The two took their positions, while Thomas tried once more to lower that iron wall. It seemed pretty shaky right now. He tried not to look at the stillness of Hugh Connor's face. Tried not to remember being six years old and feeling all grown up because Dad and Hugh had decided he was big enough to go trout fishing with them.

A trickle of sweat ran from his brow and stung his eye. Thomas blinked it away, wriggled a neck brace beneath Hugh, fastened it tight. Steadied his control, distanced himself.

He gave the signal. Men braced their shoulders and tractors growled with effort. The burden lifted. "Hold it there!" Thomas had to shout over the bellowing motors. He worked the backboard under Hugh, careful not to twist the man's body or move his spine. He had to be careful, take his time, do it right. Right out of the textbook. It was part of the job, and the fact that he knew old Hugh would rather be dead than paralyzed didn't even enter into it. The stubborn old goat. He still went fishing in the spring. Thomas had gone with him this year. Dad, too, Hugh had quietly insisted. If only in spirit.

Fastening the straps, focusing on each move he made in order to block the human side of him from interfering, Thomas carefully pulled Hugh away from the tractor that hovered above him. By the time he'd done it, the chopper was settling noisily into the field.

"Someone drive Shelly and the boys to the hospital. And go and get their pickup from my house," Thomas called over his shoulder as he helped move Hugh on board. He knew the neighbors would take care of things. Sumac, Iowa, was that kind of place. Hugh Connor's wheat would get harvested. His family would have plenty of support, a little too much company and probably a half dozen of Eugenia Overton's casseroles before tomorrow was out. They were a close-knit community, a family. A member of which Thomas steadfastly refused to become.

It was midnight by the time he got back home. One of the neighbors—he didn't know which one—had driven his Jeep to the hospital and left the keys at the nurses' station. He wasn't sure why. Not out of friendly feelings for him, that much was certain. The residents of Sumac didn't much like Thomas these days. Oh, they'd liked him well enough before... before he'd gone away and served his time in hell. He supposed they'd expected the starry-eyed kid who'd left here, not the cold stranger who'd returned. But that was their problem, not his. And if they didn't like him, at least they had a healthy respect for him. Maybe even a little fear. The man they saw as unfriendly and intimidating was in fact only keeping true to the lessons of Karicau. How many of those sweet people had he let himself care about, only to see them die? Father Elton, the village priest, picked off by a sniper while helping to distribute the latest shipment from the Red Cross. Young, pregnant Maria, blown to unrecognizable bits after stepping on a land mine. Little Alena. He closed his eyes when he thought of her huge brown ones and her bright smile. She'd been the first baby Thomas had ever delivered solo. Alena lived to the ripe old age of eight before she was peppered with shrapnel by guerrillas intent on destroying supply trucks that had just rolled into the village.

There had been more, many more Karicauans whom Thomas had become close to, hell, even loved, and who had died at the hands of the bloody revolt. And with every one who'd passed, he'd fought the despair, the sense of having failed in his mission, the horrible, gut-wrenching guilt that he—a doctor—had been unable to help them. Until, gradually, the truth had been driven into his brain like a fence post into the soft Iowa ground, being hammered down deep with a twenty-pound maul. You couldn't allow yourself to care.

Here, though, it was different.

Hugh had a cracked sternum, eight broken ribs, a punctured lung and quite a bit of internal bleeding, but he was stable now. He was going to be all right. Thomas had been relieved and glad to let Dr. Monroe handle the surgery. He never operated anymore if he could help it. It was a little harder to be distant with a patient's vital organs literally in the palms of your hands. So he just bowed out of the OR, and so far, that seemed just fine with the staff at St. Luke's.

Thomas was exhausted. Not just from the work, but from the effort of keeping his distance. It hadn't been an effort in a very long time. Closing himself off emotionally had not been a luxury on Karicau, it had been a damned necessity. Like breathing. You either learned to go cold as ice and stay that way, or you ended up in a rubber room somewhere, weaving baskets for a living. And doing it hadn't been easy. Hell, for a while he'd mourned every dead child, grieved every young mother's burial. But it hadn't gone on. He couldn't have let it go on.

So why, if he'd been able to close off his emotions in the face of the most senseless mayhem imaginable, was it so difficult to do the same here now?

Maybe because *here* was where the emotional side of him was born and raised. Hell, he sometimes thought the right half of his brain had stayed behind when he'd gone overseas. That part of him that had dreamed of castles and dragons, believed in Santa Claus, imagined beautiful princesses from distant

galaxies. It was that same part of him that seemed to
have been waiting in ambush when he'd returned six
months ago. Every breath of Sumac air seemed to in-
stigate a memory, a rush of feeling, nostalgia, something. He'd been fighting it ever since he'd come back
here, and it was difficult.

Difficult, not impossible. He'd just have to try
harder.

He slammed the door behind him, tossed the bag
into its customary spot and eyed his latest missed meal
with regret. The plate sat on the table where he'd left
it, but it was devoid of any sign of tuna casserole. He
crooked an eyebrow, lowering his gaze to the dog under the table. Humphrey just wagged his shaggy tail
and tried to look innocent.

"Didn't matter. I wasn't hungry anyway."

Humphrey barked once and lowered his head to rest
on his outstretched paws, pretending to close his eyes.
Only he kept peering out as Thomas cleared the dishes
from the table and stacked them in the dishwasher.
The dog knew he could be in big trouble for eating
from the table. Lucky for Humphrey, his master was
too tired to worry about it.

Thomas dragged himself upstairs for a quick shower
and fell into bed. But even as tired as he was, sleep
didn't come easily. The damned house was too big for
one man and a dog. Too empty, too quiet. Especially
at night, without a single sound other than the bois-
terous crickets outside. He told himself for the hun-
dredth time that he ought to sell it, move into the
vacant rooms above the clinic in town. Right between
the John Deere dealer and the feed store. It wasn't as
if he needed all this room or ever would. He had about

as much intention of settling down with a woman and raising a family as he did of running for president. Of course, he'd change his mind in a hurry if the single ladies of Sumac had their way. It was a shame he had to disappoint them. But he had nothing inside him to give to a woman. He might have had once. But whatever there had been had died in the middle of a bloody revolution. It had died just a little bit with every small child, no matter how thoroughly he'd closed off his heart. It had died of starvation and disease and war. There was no resurrecting it.

So he ought to sell. He didn't run the farm anymore. His practice kept him too busy for that, but he didn't let the land sit idle, either. He rented the fields to neighboring farmers, who grew bumper crops on it. One of them would be more than happy to own the whole place.

It was that emotional part of him that kept him from going ahead and selling the place. He might have managed to exorcise the boy inside him, to be rid of him the entire time he'd spent away from here in hell. But the kid still lived in this house. Everywhere on this damned farm. And *he* was the one who kept Thomas from selling out. To that boy, this place was magic. It spurred the kinds of dreams and fantasies that seemed too real not to believe in. Made a kid feel like a hero, rescuing strange and beautiful damsels on Iowa summer nights.

God, had he ever been that young? That naive and gullible? Believed in such utter nonsense? Had such crazy dreams? Didn't seem possible when he thought about it now.

He closed his eyes, knowing good and well there'd be no dreams, no childish fantasies. He never dreamed anymore, with the exception of a few occasional nightmares.

It was 5:45 when the odd buzzing sensation woke him up. His eyes opened, bleary and unfocused. But it grew louder, and he sat up in bed as his head cleared, reaching for the light. It was still there. Buzzing, like a hive of bees, only it was coming from inside. Inside *him*. He thought of tinnitus and smacked the side of his head with his palm, but the sound didn't go away. For just a moment, he remembered what that sensation had signified in his youth.

"Ah, bull. That wasn't real. . . ."

But something drew him and he got up. He pulled on his jeans and went to the window.

"This is stupid. This is utterly—" The buzzing grew louder. "Stupid." He pushed the window open and stood for a minute staring up at the sky. He shook his head at the insane urge to climb out, the way he used to do. He glanced down at the trellis, knowing damn well that such a ridiculous effort would probably be good for one big laugh and several broken bones.

There was a simple explanation for the sound. And he would sure as hell find out what it was and put a stop to it so he could get a few hours' sleep. He glanced down, and realized that his hand was absently rubbing the oval-shaped charm he wore on a chain around his neck. He forced his hand down.

But the buzzing sound grew still louder.

He snapped his jeans, tugging the zipper up as he trotted down the stairs. Then he stopped at another sound, a growl. Humphrey stood poised as if for attack near the door. His upper lip curled away from his teeth; his tail pointed straight in the air, nearly vibrating.

Thomas frowned. "What is it, boy? Somebody out there who shouldn't be?" Humphrey didn't change position until Thomas caught him by the collar and tugged him away from the door. Then Thomas opened it, slipped outside and closed it again before his wannabe-rottweiller could escape and do someone bodily harm.

His bare feet hit the cool damp grass, and memories rushed over him. Running through the wheat fields, warm summer breezes in his hair, eager young eyes scanning the night sky for...

Hell, he'd been a little kid with a big imagination. And the charm around his neck ... well, he'd probably found it in the woods on one of his excursions. His mind had concocted a fantasy around it. Or his subconscious had woven a dream to explain its presence. He'd had a notoriously vivid dream life as a kid.

So why have you been wearing it ever since, then? Huh?

Thomas scowled at the childlike voice inside his head, forcibly ignoring its sarcastic question. Walking a little ways in the dewy grass, he looked around. The buzzing still sounded in his ears, but he saw no explanation for it. Maybe he was dreaming now. He couldn't be sure. And just because he'd stopped dreaming didn't mean his mind couldn't have decided to start up again. It didn't *feel* like a dream, though. The night breeze was real. The muscles in his shoulders and back ached from tension and his head throbbed a little. He wouldn't feel that in a dream, would he? His stomach growled and he remembered that he hadn't eaten.

"Okay, maybe it's not a dream. I'm out here like an idiot, in the middle of the night. Something is buzzing, and my dog doesn't like it any better than I do. So what the hell is going on?"

A little thrill of excitement raced up the back of his neck, the way it used to when he was a kid. He caught it, balled it up in a mental fist and tossed it away. There was no reason for it. He wasn't a kid anymore. And this wasn't one of his childhood fantasies.

He stood there a minute, staring up at the empty sky, wondering what sane man would be out here shirtless and shoeless in the middle of the night after the day he'd put in. Why the hell had he come outside, anyway? And why hadn't that buzzing in his head faded in the least now that the cool night air was slapping his face, bringing him more awake and alert than ever?

A blinding green glow cut a swath through the sky. It arced from somewhere high and east, curving downward like a big green rainbow, only to disappear just beyond the treeline in the distance. Thomas felt the ground rock with a soundless impact.

"Holy..." He stared for a second, shocked motionless.

Something seemed to slam into him from behind, some invisible force, propelling him forward. Stupid to run like this! Stupid, foolish, utterly senseless. He hadn't seen anything. Not really. Maybe the stress from his time on Karicau had finally caught up to him. Maybe this was some sort of breakdown. He told himself all those things, but still his legs strained, air burned in and out of his lungs, his feet hammered the ground in rhythm with his pulse.

It wasn't as far for a grown man as it had seemed to a ten-year-old boy. He crossed the field, the stubble of recently cut wheat stabbing at the soles of his feet. A grown man ought to know enough to wear shoes. How many times had Dad told him that? *Thomas Allan, you're gonna lose a foot if you don't start wearing shoes when you go out.*

For a second he'd heard that deep, booming voice speaking close to his ears. But it hadn't been real. Just those damned memories sneaking up on him again, trying to claim him.

The field behind him, he splashed across the stream, soaking his jeans up to his calves. He ran through the knee-high grass, up onto the little knoll and right on over. His heart pounding so hard he could hear it, he loped into the woods, over the uneven, damp ground, toward the clearing he remembered so well. That magical, secret meadow.

He saw a silent explosion when he got there. The shape—that same glowing green spider shape he remembered—simply glowed bright white and vanished. Nothing remained. Nothing. He briefly imagined the headline in the tiny *Sumac Daily Star*. "Local Doctor Suffers Mental Breakdown In Woods."

But something *had been* there. The ground was charred black, completely barren. Not a single blade of grass stood in the steaming circle of earth. And the buzzing in his head was gone.

He heard a groan, and his spine went rigid. He turned very slowly, walked without seeing, still blinded by that brilliant *imaginary* flash of light.

She lay on the ground, her black hair covering her face. She wasn't moving. Thomas knelt beside her. Maybe "knelt" wasn't the right word. His knees sort of buckled under him, landing him on the ground. He reached out, touched her, as if to be sure she was real.

And then the wall slammed down, saving his sanity yet again. His hands moved automatically, checking for broken bones, slipping under her to feel her spine, touching her neck, feeling the soft beat of her pulse beneath warm skin. He pushed the hair away from her face.

Her huge, slanted eyes opened, and she stared at him. She blinked, one hand rising weakly, touching the amulet he wore. Her lips parted. "Thom...us..." The beautiful eyes closed again, and she lay still.

He stared down at her, unable to believe what he was seeing as his vision slowly came back. Around her neck, suspended on a thin, silvery chain, hung a slingshot. He touched it, felt his initials carved into the handle. "Janella," he whispered. "My God, Janella...."

Chapter 2

She was light. Too light, maybe. Or maybe his imagination was kicking in.

Oh, yeah, start worrying about your imagination, Doc. You're carrying a semiconscious alien woman away from the spot where her frigging mothership just vaporized. I'd say that's as good a time as any to worry about the old imagination. Maybe ought to give a thought to the sanity while you're at it, don't you think?

It was too ridiculous even to contemplate. Impossible. Things like this happened in childhood fantasies, not in the real adult world. So it wasn't happening. It couldn't be. He'd probably wake up in bed and laugh about it.

The silky material of her blouse rubbing against his bare chest was too real to be a dream, though. The heat of her body suffusing his. That soft cheek rest-

ing on his shoulder. Hair like black satin, trailing
down his arm. Her soft breath, whispering near his
neck.

Ah, hell, it was all real. He knew damned well it
was, no matter how little sense it made. He figured if
he was going to fantasize, he'd have had her awake
and healthy, not suffering from God knows what
kinds of injuries. He wasn't even sure he could help
her.

That thought brought him up short. He swore under his breath as he searched her face. Then he averted
his gaze, but a little too late. That bronzed skin,
bathed in moonlight, the turned-up nose, those long
black lashes had already imbedded themselves in his
mind. She was small, delicate, helpless, depending on
him to get her through this. He closed his eyes for a
second, trying to tug down that iron wall that kept him
emotionally removed. But it wasn't easy. Always before he'd felt sure of himself, competent. He'd known
he could do what needed doing, help any patient who
wasn't beyond helping. But he didn't *know how* to
help her. He couldn't check her vitals, because he
didn't know what they ought to be. He couldn't ad-
minister medication without knowing what reactions
it might cause in her. She looked human, but—if this
wasn't a dream—she wasn't. Was she?

This was beyond his area of expertise. He ought to
call someone. Somewhere in the world there must be
someone who'd know what to do for her.

You can't tell anyone, and you know it.

He opened his eyes and exhaled slowly. Damn, that
was the voice of a little boy lecturing him, not one of
reason. He ought to call someone—

You promised!

"I never promised anything." Great. Now he was whispering to himself as he carried her back through the woods toward home.

You did so. In your mind, your heart, you swore you'd never tell.

The irritating young voice had a point there. He had sort of promised. But at the time he'd considered it more a vow to himself than to anyone else. And he still wasn't sure why he'd felt so strongly about it, especially since the secret he'd sworn to keep had only existed inside his own mind.

Or maybe not.

You have to help her. She's depending on you.

What was so new about that? People were always depending on him, pinning their hopes on him as if he were some kind of god instead of just a man with a medical degree. But that's all he was. And he didn't have any more saintly qualities, any more compassion or caring, than the next guy did. Maybe less. Show me a doctor who cares and I'll show you a basket case waiting to happen. That had always been his philosophy.

But this is different. You have to care this time. Look at her!

"Shut up," he muttered to the boyish voice in his mind. But it was too late. He was already looking at her, remembering the lost little girl, the fear in her eyes, the tears.

Those same eyes opened now, blinked up at him, and he stopped walking for a second. She smiled slightly, lifted a hand to touch his face. "I knew you'd come, Thomas. I knew..." The hand fell again as her eyes fluttered closed.

"Ah, hell," Thomas murmured, resuming the brisk pace.

He emerged from the woods onto the grassy slope and picked up his pace a little more. He splashed through the stream and crossed the stubble-covered wheat field, no longer noticing the pokes in his feet. She stirred a little, moaned softly. One hand came up to clasp his neck and his hold on her tightened automatically.

He crossed the lawn, kicked the front door opened and came face-to-face with Eugenia Overton and her endlessly curious eyes. Hands on her slender hips, she gaped at him, then at the woman in his arms.

"Thomas Allan Duffy, what in the name of heaven are you up to?"

Humphrey lunged out from under the table, barking and snarling in a way Thomas had never seen him do. The black-and-white fur on his haunches bristled and his teeth were bared. Janella's eyes flew wide and she screamed loudly enough to wake a coma patient. Her arms snagged Thomas's neck. She cringed closer to him, damn near cutting off his airway. She screamed again, louder.

"It's all right!" He turned, putting his back to Humphrey, but the dog kept barking and Janella kept screaming. "Dammit, Eugenia, grab the dog!"

Eugenia had already done just that. She had Humphrey by his collar, smacking him repeatedly on the nose with her other hand, as she tugged him into the small pantry and shut the door. When she turned to face Thomas again she was breathless. One strand of copper-red hair hung down over her pinkened face.

She blew the hair away with an exasperated puff. "Well? You going to tell me what's going on?"

Janella still clung to him, shaking all over. Hot tears dampened his neck where her face was buried. So what? he asked himself. Hell, it wasn't as if he hadn't seen patients cry before.

Yeah. You've seen her cry before. And it made your stomach churn then, too.

Shut the hell up!

But his hold on Janella tightened a little more, and one of his hands had apparently decided it was necessary to stroke her hair. He stopped it, glanced at Eugenia. "No, as a matter of fact, I'm not. So go home."

Pushing past Eugenia, he carried Janella through the kitchen, into the living room and upstairs into his bedroom. He wondered briefly whether her clothes had given her away to his neighbor. Outside, he hadn't really noticed what she was wearing.

Thank God, he thought, no silver lamé. The blouse looked like silk, but felt a lot heavier, sturdier. It didn't appear all that unusual, full sleeves with tighter cuffs. A fitted waist. High, snug collar. The pants reminded him of spandex, and both were black. She wore ankle-high boots of buttery-soft, leatherlike material.

He tugged the covers back with one hand, then bent to lower her into the bed. She stared into his eyes, hers huge and frightened, her hands still clasped tight at the base of his neck. He reached behind him and gently tugged her hands away so he could straighten. She blinked in apparent confusion, but lay back on his pillows.

A bang made her go stiff. Thomas whirled to see Eugenia standing by the window.

"What the heck did you leave that open for? It's not exactly warm outside. And on a similar note, where's your shirt? You're a doctor, for crying out loud. Don't you know better than—"

"Eugenia, what the hell are you doing in my bedroom at six in the morning?"

That shut her up. She pursed her pretty lips and frowned, and he took a second to notice that no matter when you saw Eugenia she was perfectly made up and beautiful. Single, too. Sumac's own Miss Kitty. All she needed was some big strong Marshal Dillon to come along and sweep her off her feet. Then she'd stop worrying so much about his chronic bachelorhood. Maybe.

"So?" He prodded, wishing like hell she'd take her good intentions and leave. "What did you bring this time? A carrot cake or another prospective wife for me?"

She pulled herself up taller, obviously insulted. "I saw an explosion. Or at least it looked like one. There didn't seem to be any noise along with it. It seemed to be coming from this way, so naturally I had to come over and make sure you were all right."

"Naturally."

"Don't try that nasty attitude on me, Thomas. You know I'm the only one in town who doesn't buy it."

"Are you, now?" He turned back to his patient, pushed her hair away from her face and saw the swollen, rapidly bruising spot just above her temple.

"You know I am. Everyone else shakes in their boots when you glower at them that way. But I'm not scared of you. Not one bit."

"Maybe you ought to be." He leaned closer to Janella, touched the spot gently, decided she might have a slight concussion at the most. It ought to be all right.

"Don't you forget, Thomas, I knew you before you went away. You weren't so intimidating when you were in my ninth-grade English class."

"People change." He turned, intending to go downstairs for his medical bag. But Eugenia had apparently grabbed it on the way up. She slung it hard into his chest.

"Not really," she muttered.

Thomas snapped open the bag, took out a cold pack and crushed it in his hand to activate it. When he felt the chill working into his palm, he laid the pack carefully over the lump on Janella's head. She only watched him, wide-eyed, glancing every few seconds at Eugenia. Thomas reached down, clasping her wrist in gentle fingers, feeling her pulse, glancing at the second hand on the clock beside the bed, wondering why the hell he bothered when he had no idea what would be normal for her. Still, the strong, steady thrum against his fingers reassured him.

"This lady was in some kind of accident, I take it. That must have been what I saw."

Damn woman wouldn't be put off easily. "I guess so," he agreed.

"What about her car? Did you find that?"

"No sign of it." Thomas licked his lips. "She said she was alone, though, so we don't need to be in a big rush to go looking for it. No chance of any other victims."

"Couldn't be much left of it anyway, after an explosion like that," Eugenia added. She tilted her head, perusing the woman on the bed as she circled it, stopping on the opposite side. "Well, someone ought to call her folks. She must have family." She leaned over Janella, who seemed to cringe deeper into the sheets. "What's your name, hon? Where are you from?"

Janella's eyes widened, her gaze darting from Eugenia back to Thomas.

"Look, Eugenia, you came to check things out. You've done that. Now, if you don't mind, I have a patient to tend to. One who's not in any shape for the third degree. Okay?"

Eugenia sniffed indignantly, tossed her coppery head. "You don't scare me, Thomas Duffy." Her gaze moved back to Janella, and softened. "I'll come back tomorrow. Maybe she'll want some company by then." She turned and hurried out the door, down the stairs. He heard her car start up and move away a few seconds later, and sighed in relief.

"Thomas . . ."

He turned quickly, scanning Janella's face. She touched her forearm lightly. "I have pain," she whispered.

Ah, hell. The wall, dammit. Bring down the wall.

He schooled his expression to remain blank and dipped into the bag for a pair of scissors. Sitting on the edge of the bed, he lifted her arm, his touch utterly impersonal, while she watched him, eyes wide, curious, but not frightened. Holding the cuff of her sleeve, he slipped the scissor blade inside and began to cut it away. Only, the stuff didn't cut. Frowning, he tried again, until her hand closed over his, and she shook her head. "Very strong." She touched the blouse as she said it. "It will not tear."

Right. Okay, so I'm treating an alien with an injured arm, and she's wearing some material that can't be cut. No big deal. Just quit thinking about it and concentrate on the job.

She sat up, lifting one hand to the front of the blouse where there was no visible seam or button or zipper. She hooked a forefinger inside the neck and easily pulled the blouse open down the front.

Thomas knew he ought to be really amazed at this new, invisible fastener that seemed to seal the material together like magic. But he was too busy noticing the creamy swell of her breasts where the shirt fell open. He was a doctor, for crying out loud. He did not notice breasts unless there was something wrong with them.

She shrugged out of the blouse, completely unembarrassed, it seemed. She very carefully peeled it from her injured arm and lay back, fully revealed from the waist up. No, there was definitely nothing wrong with them. And he was noticing them anyway, and wondering where the hell his damned professional disinterest had hidden itself.

She frowned and held up her injured arm. "It *hurts.*"

Her voice had an air of command he didn't much like. Ah, terrific, something about her he *didn't* like. Aside from her being from outer space, of course. He closed his eyes and gave his head a shake. He'd just

about given up the idea that he'd wake up in the
morning to find none of this had been real. Maybe he
ought to try to wake up now, though, just for the hell
of it. He focused on lucidity, on full awareness, and
popped his eyes open.

No good. She still lay on his bed, and her breasts
were still perfect and firm and entirely exposed, right
to their dark centers and puckering nipples.

Thomas swallowed hard and pulled the covers over
her distractions for the time being. He took the slingshot from around her neck and put it in its old spot—
the drawer beside the bed. "I can't believe you kept it
all this time."

She blinked at him. "Why? You kept the amulet,
didn't you?"

"Yeah, but—"

"I knew we'd meet again. It was fate, Thomas."

Wondering what she meant by that pronouncement
made him uncomfortable, so he changed the subject
back to the matter at hand. He examined the forearm. "It's broken. I'll have to put a cast on it."

She tilted her head. "Cast?"

"It's all right. It will feel better when I'm finished." He reached for his bag, fished out the soft
gauze and then the plaster bandages, setting them on
the nightstand. Then he went to the bathroom and ran
a basin of hot water. He brought it back to the bedside, dropped the plaster rolls into it.

He had to set the bone first. He took her arm in
both hands, met her gaze, and his stomach clenched a
little at the thought of hurting her. That shouldn't
have happened. He shouldn't have *let* it happen. "This
is going to hurt, Janella. But only for a second."

"Pain is not good, Thomas. I do not like it."

"I have to do it, or the arm won't heal."

She frowned. "You are a healer?"

"Yes."

"You are certain?"

For crying out loud. Did she want to see his license to practice? "I'm certain."

She stared at him for a moment, some kind of wonder in her eyes. Then her jaw firmed up, and she repeated, "I dislike pain." Nonetheless she closed her eyes, braced herself.

Thomas snapped the bone into place and she screamed. Her eyes squeezed tighter and moisture seeped onto her thick lashes. He grated his teeth and refused to look at her face. "I'm sorry. It'll be better soon, I promise." She opened her eyes, glared at him for a second, then relaxed against the pillows as if resigned.

He began wrapping the soft cotton around her forearm, then the gauze. "Can you tell me where you come from, Janella?" He finished with the gauze and fished a roll of plaster out of the warm water.

She glanced toward his window, toward the sky. "Far away. I do not know how to say the name in your language." Her eyes seemed so sad.

"How do you even know my language?"

She brought her gaze back to his. "We know *all* your languages." She had to think about it before she finished. "We've always known."

Thomas nodded, deciding all of a sudden he didn't really want to hear this. His brain had taken in enough insanity tonight to put it on overload.

"I couldn't stay there," she muttered, as if to herself.

He frowned, pausing in his ministrations to search her face, then wished he hadn't. She was hurting, and not just physically.

"Why not?" Ah, hell, hadn't he just decided he didn't want to know?

She only shook her head.

Okay, so she got into some kind of trouble up there on Krypton or wherever the hell she came from, and she'd swiped a handy UFO—the glowing green model was hot this season—and made a getaway to planet Earth.

Yup, and the moon is made of green cheese, too. Come on, next do you suppose she'll ask you to take her to your leader?

"Earth is better for me."

Uh-huh, makes perfect sense. You're having a breakdown, Duffy. A major one.

Thomas began winding the warm, wet plaster around her arm, smoothing it very slowly. She closed her eyes, and he knew the warmth was soothing her pain a little.

"But my ship failed, and I could not regain control."

"And you crashed. You must have been thrown clear before—"

"The ship is gone." Her eyes squeezed tighter and she cleared her throat. "I can not change my mind now. I can never go back."

"Was there anyone else with you?" He immediately thought of going back out, searching the area for other survivors. It was ludicrous, but...

"I'm alone," she whispered.

His heart twisted a little in his chest. Thomas ordered it to freeze in place and stay the hell out of this. "You're not alone, Janella. You have a friend, hmm? One from your childhood."

She sniffed, and stared at him, smiling just a little. "Yes. One friend. One trusted friend who will keep our secret." Her eyes took on a determined gleam. "No one must know about me, Thomas. Not ever." Again that air of command.

He finished the cast. "Hell, no one would believe me if I told them." He rinsed his hands in the water. It felt real, wet the way water should. Wouldn't things be more distorted if this were a mental crisis of some kind? "But don't worry, I'm not going to. You can trust me." He took her chin in his hand, fought a brief battle with his own eyes, which seemed inclined to linger on her mouth, and turned her head slightly. "Now, let me take a look at your head."

In the secret air base in Groom Lake, Nevada, alarms went off and lights flashed. An alien vessel had entered Earth's atmosphere, and apparently crashed in the U.S.A. The tracking systems went into action, putting the crash site somewhere in the state of Iowa. That was all they got before the vessel apparently disintegrated. Still, the team was dispatched. UFO sightings from that area would get immediate attention, and they'd track down and recover any bodies or wreckage before too many people asked too many questions. They'd put the locals' minds to rest with cover stories of weather balloons or air-force test flights. They'd bring any evidence that was to be

found back to Groom Lake, where it would be ana-
lyzed, studied and then stored under armed guard in
hangar thirty-five. The entire investigation and the
cover-up would go off like clockwork.

They always did.

Thomas's hands were soothing and gentle on her
arm, as he administered the ancient remedy for a broken bone. And soft again when he examined the
painful bump on her head. He remained bare chested,
and she studied him openly and well, not nearly as
afraid now as she had been earlier.

She cringed inwardly when she thought of the fear
she'd displayed so openly in front of him. What must
he think of her, giving vent to her emotions that way?
But then she reminded herself that things were different here. And that this was why she'd come. She
wasn't worthy of the life laid out for her at home. And
she'd often wondered if the blood of the ruling class
truly ran in her veins, or if there had been some mix-up
to explain her parentage. She was nothing like them.
Nothing. She *felt* things. Many things. So many, she
envisioned a cauldron somewhere inside her, one
bubbling over with emotions and passions. All the
things forbidden to her, the things no true ruler was
supposed to feel.

"Emotions make you weak, Janella." How many
times had her mother whispered those words to her.
"They interfere with one's ability to think clearly,
make practical decisions. Look at the wars and tur-
moil on Earth. *That* is where emotions will get you."

Janella shook her head, remembering. Her father
had traces of emotion—to her mother's constant cha-

grin. Nothing like Janella's explosive feelings, of course. But when his own father had grown feeble and old, and the women of the ruling house had added the old man's name to the list of those to be euthanized at the annual ceremony, he'd defied them all. Janella was secretly proud of that. Her father, Matalin, had smuggled Grandfather aboard what was supposed to be a routine reconnaissance ship. And Janella, the only person who knew his plans, had sneaked aboard, as well.

It had been a wonderful adventure, orbiting Earth, searching for the perfect place for Grandfather to live out his waning years. Until he'd died. He'd succumbed just as they'd landed in the woods behind this place. And as Matalin had buried him there, Janella, overcome with grief, had run off into the trees. When her grief was spent, she'd been unable to find her way back to her father and the ship.

And then Thomas had found her.

She closed her eyes, remembering that night as clearly as if it had been yesterday. Thomas had been young, but so strong and confident. He'd reminded her of the heroes in the old stories, the men from days gone by. Men of courage and honor, in the times before the ruling house had taken control of the planet. She'd fallen in love with Thomas that night. She'd known then that she would hold his image in her heart forever.

She'd secretly despised the ruling house since her return, and had always intended to flee them before her time to serve as one of them came to pass. For the crime of trying to rescue his father, Matalin had been sentenced to spend the rest of his life in prison. Her father must have known what his fate would be, but he'd returned all the same. He'd been determined to use his trial as a forum, to speak out against the system and the ruling house. Janella had only seen him once after his judgment had been passed, just before he'd been taken to the ship bound for the prison planet. And his words to her still rang in her ears.

"You don't belong here, Janella. No more than I do. You're not like them. You never can be. When you're grown, leave them. Go to Earth, as I should have done long ago. Go there and find happiness. You will. I know you will."

Well, she'd heeded her father's words. She'd come here. She'd made it safely, only to find a woman who seemed far too interested in her business, and a noisy creature with far too many sharp teeth. And Thomas. A healer. Of all things, he'd become a healer. There'd been no healers at home, excepting for the few who practiced illegally in darkened, hidden rooms. If caught practicing, they would pay with their lives. The ruling house had determined there was no longer a need for healers. It was impractical to spend time and resources on illness. Simple injuries were healed with no more than an injection. The seriously ill, those born with abnormalities or disease, the old and infirm, were gathered together once a year for the ritual euthanasia. This way only the strong and healthy survived, to bear more strong and healthy offspring.

It was a system Janella had never accepted, and her explosive temper and impulsive nature had landed her in trouble over it more than once.

Her father had been right. She was never meant to live among them. She'd long ago decided she was meant to be here. With Thomas.

Thomas put the cold square back on her head, leaning over her as he pressed the frigid thing gently to her bump. His chest was smooth and rippled with strength. She'd never seen its like. The men of her world were dim reflections of him. Soft, flabby. But then, they were of little importance, anyway. No one much cared what they looked like.

She'd thought of Thomas often since he'd rescued her so long ago. She'd known he was trustworthy even then. Rare for a male. Even more odd that she should be here depending on one to help her. But even in adulthood, he didn't seem like the conquered men from her world.

She'd been right about Thomas. He'd rescued her again, tonight. Somehow, she'd known he'd be here for her. And her likening of him to one of the legendary heroes had been correct, as well. His skin bore the kiss of the sun, and the body that skin covered was broad and hard.

She lifted one hand and laid her palm against his chest. Warm, firm. She liked it, and ran her hand over it from side to side and down over his rippled abdomen. He looked down at her, frowning.

"You're very hard," she observed, letting her hand fall away for the moment.

"If you only knew," he said, and he was smiling.

She liked his smile, also. But it vanished all too quickly, to be replaced by the harsh, hardened expression he seemed to favor.

"Are all men here that way?"

He shook his head. "It comes from hard work."

She nodded. So men here still acted as laborers. No doubt their primitive technology left much that still needed physical strength to accomplish.

She tilted her head. "We have writings... stories of the heroes of old. They are described much like you. Hard and strong." She reached up, ran her hand over his chest again and nodded. "I approve of it."

The corners of his lips turned upward, as if he would like to smile again, but he resisted the urge. His mouth took on a thin line and his jaw seemed to clamp firmly.

That creature with the sharp teeth and angry voice bellowed from below, and she gasped. She barely restrained herself from huddling under the covers. Instead, she drowned her fear in righteous indignation, and then anger. If that beast came near her again she'd send it flying into the nearest wall!

Thomas's hand closed around hers, removing it from his chest as if her touch disturbed him. That made her still angrier. "It's all right, Janella. It's just my dog."

"I do *not* like *dog*. You will take it away from here."

"No, I don't think I will."

Thomas studied her face, replacing the fallen cold thing on her head. His gaze was hard and she blinked in surprise. Was he defying her?

"The dog must go," she repeated.

"Look, honey, in case you haven't noticed yet, this is *my* house. And that is *my* dog. He's not going anywhere." He pursed his lips, as if considering something. Then he muttered a few angry words she didn't recognize and went on. "I know you're scared. But

Humphrey won't hurt you. He's just afraid of you because he doesn't know you."

"*He's* afraid of *me*?"

Thomas nodded. "I won't let him near you until you're ready, but believe me, he's a good dog."

She sat up a little. The thing on her arm was getting hard and heavy, but the soreness had eased a little. She met Thomas's eyes, a bit confused at his refusal to comply with her command. Still, she supposed, she could give him a bit of leeway, since he'd rescued her twice in her lifetime and since he was destined to be her mate, as she'd known for many years.

She lifted her chin, though, and made her words very firm and clear. "If he bites me with those teeth, I will pull them all out."

"He won't bite you."

She sulked, but settled back on the bed. She was very tired, which surprised her. She should be too curious about this strange place and this man to think of sleep. She supposed the effort of traveling so far and her injuries were draining her energy.

She blinked, recalling for a moment all those she'd left behind. People, family, friends whom she'd loved. But they hadn't wanted her love, anyway. And they allowed themselves to feel none for her in return. She couldn't have lived there much longer. She felt she'd have withered and died in the attempt. It will be better here, she told herself. Then, glancing at the hard, emotionless eyes of the man at her side, she wondered. Would it be better here? Or had she simply exchanged one unbearable life for another?

Her eyelids drooped. Janella yawned and rested her head on the pillows.

"That's good. You get some sleep. I'll be just down the hall if you need anything." He started to move toward the door. She sat up and slammed it shut.

Thomas stood very still near the door, just staring at it. Then he turned to stare at her. "How in the hell did you do that?"

She frowned, uncertain what was confusing him so much. "I will rest better if you stay with me, Thomas." She used a smile to soften the harsh, commanding tone of her words.

He gave his head a shake, scowling darkly for a second. He looked from her to the door and back again. Then shrugged as his expression softened, just slightly. "Yeah, okay. I can do that. I suppose you're afraid to be alone right now." He came back to her, sat down in the chair beside the bed.

She shook her head and threw back the covers with her good arm. "Here, with me. I will sleep very well with my head upon your hard chest, I think."

He seemed so surprised. His gaze affixed itself to her breasts and remained there for a very long time. So long she wondered if he saw something wrong with them.

She looked down, puzzled. "What is it, Thomas? Are they not as beautiful as the breasts of your women?" She glanced up at him again, thoroughly confused.

His gaze rose to meet hers and he opened his mouth, but only stammered for a moment. Finally he pushed a hand through his lovely brown hair. So soft and long. She liked that, too.

"Around here, women tend to keep them covered up. Especially in front of men."

She puckered her brows harder. "That is archaic." She looked at her breasts again. "But they aren't lacking in any way?"

He pursed his lips and looked at her chest for a long moment. "No, they're not lacking."

She smiled, relieved at that. She couldn't have the females of this planet thinking her inferior. Then she looked at his hair-sprinkled chest, at the smoky quartz stone he still wore, and chewed her lip. "Yours are not covered."

"Well . . . that's different."

"In what way?"

He closed his eyes and let his chin fall until it touched his chest. "It just is. You'll understand once you've been here awhile." He turned from her, dug through a basket and emerged with a soft shirt. He handed it to her. "Here. If I'm spending what's left of the night with you, you'd better put this T-shirt on."

She licked her lips. "I think you will have to put it on for me." She glanced down at her useless arm, weighed down by the heavy cast he'd put on it. He nodded and stepped forward, stretched the shirt over her head and eased her injured arm through. She noticed he took great care not to touch her skin any more than was necessary. Was he afraid she carried some kind of disease?

When he finished, she lay back on the bed. "I do not usually wear clothing to bed," she complained.

"Yeah, well, neither do I. Guess we'll both have to make an exception tonight. And I'll stay in the chair."

He sat back down where he'd been and she scowled at him. He'd defied her, and for the second time to-night. He was taking his role as legendary hero a bit too literally. Those men, she'd heard, had been free thinkers, independent, too strong to be ruled by their women. Could he be more like them than she'd imagined?

She wondered about that as she settled back in the bed. She found she was quite disgusted with him a second later when, instead of undressing, he pulled a blanket over himself, covering that wonderful chest. She'd been very eager to see what he looked like completely uncovered. She rolled over and punched the pillow. When he chuckled softly, she only got angrier.

Chapter 3

It was a clean break. And the head injury wasn't serious. Her physical injuries no longer worried him. It was her lack of shyness that he was concerned about now. Okay, so maybe her society didn't impose the same conventions as his did. So what the hell was his moral obligation? He'd have loved to crawl into bed with her half-naked. But he knew better. Maybe she didn't have moral burdens to carry. Hell, he didn't, either. Not really.

But he didn't want any entanglements with any women. Physical needs were easily satisfied. A woman who knew just what she was doing and expected nothing in return was pretty much his method, and it worked just fine. But not some strange woman with no sense of shyness and a head injury. And certainly not a patient. No way.

So he'd just suffer the rest of the night in this chair with a hard-on a cat couldn't scratch down. Served him right, he supposed, for failing to keep himself removed.

He'd stop thinking about her luscious little body, he decided. But when he did, it was only to focus in on her huge, dark eyes and the fear that showed in them every time he looked at her, even when she was angry. When he gazed into those eyes, he saw the frightened little girl he'd found in the woods so long ago. And that made him feel like the little boy who'd rescued her and who'd wondered for the first time in his life what it would feel like to kiss a girl. But he couldn't let himself dwell on all that, either. That kid had been driving him nuts trying to get back into his head ever since he'd come home again. He didn't need to give the little pest an opening. He had a feeling his professional distance would suffer a horrendous setback if he did.

That little kid had been the one who'd decided he had to become a doctor. That little kid—the one who'd found some kind of joy beyond measure in mending the broken wings of robins and taking in every injured animal, tame or otherwise, that he came across. He'd had a knack for healing. And he'd fallen in love with the idea that helping people get well, taking care of them, was some kind of magical gift. He'd wanted a medical degree more than he'd ever wanted anything. So badly he'd traded eight years of his life away to the U.S. Army in exchange for his education. He'd seen being a doctor as something sacred, almost a calling.

He'd been wrong. It was a job just like any other job. He refused to think of it in any other terms.

Despite the look in Janella's eyes when he'd told her he was what she called a healer. She'd seemed awed, admiration gleaming from her mysterious dark eyes as she'd stared at him. She had to be the most beautiful female he'd ever come across in his life, bar none.

Damn, he was thinking about her again. Okay, he'd distract himself by considering the telekinesis.

She'd slammed that door. There'd been no draft, no sudden shift in air pressure. She'd slammed it, and she'd done it without lifting a finger. He wondered what else she could do. It was a damned good thing she hadn't exhibited that talent in front of Eugenia.

He stared at her as she fell asleep. Odd having a woman sleeping under this old roof. Hadn't been one here overnight since Dad had tossed Mother, her belongings and her booze out the door almost thirty-eight years ago. He'd been a baby then, too young to remember any of it. But he'd heard the stories. Sumac was a small town, after all.

The improbability of a woman sleeping in his bed, in his house, was exceeded only by that of a spaceship crashing in the woods and of an *alien* woman—who liked his body—sleeping in here. He decided not to think about those things, either. It wasn't an easy task. And he never did fall asleep.

She stirred just as he entered the bedroom with the trayful of food. She sat up, blinking at him, first in confusion and then in recognition. And then a deep sadness filled her eyes. She'd remembered everything she'd left behind. He knew it without her saying so, and wished he didn't. It wouldn't do to start feeling anything for her, not even sympathy.

He went into the room, sat on the edge of the bed and refused to look at her eyes.

"My arm hurts," she snapped. "Have you nothing to eliminate pain?"

He faced her then, bolstered by her bitchiness. *That* he could handle. "We have drugs, Janella, but I have no way of knowing their effects on you. They might make you sick, might even be fatal to you. You understand?"

She frowned at him. "We are the same species, Thomas. What is good for you is good for me."

He gave his head a shake. "The same species?"

She rolled her eyes as if he were stupid. "Do you think two separate species would evolve as similarly as we have? Look at me."

He did *not* want to look at her. Especially when she sat up, her breasts jiggling beneath his thin white T-shirt. So why was he looking anyway?

"We colonized Earth thousands of years ago, Thomas, when our planet became overpopulated. We all have the same ancestors somewhere along the line. Now, give me something for this pain."

"You know, for a guest in my home, you're one bossy, demanding, *rude* woman."

"Give me something!"

"No."

She blinked and he knew she was shocked speechless.

"But—"

"Janella, even if we started out the same, we may have evolved differently. There are environmental factors, things we've been exposed to that you haven't, a million other things that could lead to differences. Ones that don't show. I'll be damned if I'll give you something that could kill you."

Her anger faded from her eyes very slowly. She sighed, nodded. "You're very wise . . . for a male."

He didn't even ask what the hell that was supposed to mean.

"Are you hungry?"

She lifted her face, a slight smile playing with her lips. "Yes." Then she frowned and added, "But I have heard of the way your people feed, and I will not eat that dog."

He bit his lips. Damn, it was tough to keep a cold, wide, preferably impassable gulf between them when she kept making him want to laugh out loud. "We don't eat our dogs, Janella."

"No?"

"No."

"Other creatures, though?"

"Well, yeah, we eat meat."

"Barbaric." She eyed the tray suspiciously.

"It's just pancakes with blueberry syrup." He pointed to the steaming stack as he spoke. "This is an orange, and this is coffee. No meat. I promise."

He set the tray on her lap and she picked up a wedge of the orange. "It is fruit?"

"Yeah. Try it. But be careful, and pay attention to the way you feel. If you eat just a little of things, and slowly, we can determine whether you're going to have a reaction to any of them."

She tilted her head, studying his face. "You are being very careful with my health."

"Yeah, well, it's part of the job. Try the damned orange, will you? I don't have time to sit here all morning."

She popped the wedge of fruit into her mouth, frowning and chewing. She nodded and licked the juice from her lips. His gaze riveted itself to her mouth for a long moment before he cleared his throat and averted his eyes.

She finished the orange and sat back, waiting for a few minutes, apparently paying attention to her body for signs the fruit had not agreed with it. When she ran out of patience, she tried some of the pancakes, again nodding in approval.

"It is good. Thank you." She sipped the coffee, grimaced and set the cup down. "This I do not like."

"It's an acquired taste."

She nodded and studied him for a moment. "The female, the one you call Oogena, she will come back."

"It's Eugenia, and you're right. She'll be back. She always comes back."

"Are you her man?"

The idea surprised him so much he almost laughed again. "Hell no. Just a friend. She was close to my father, and now she thinks it's her job to keep tabs on me. She's harmless. A pain in the backside, but harmless."

Janella sighed in apparent relief. Then frowned. "Harmless. That remains to be seen. What will you tell her about me?"

"She thinks you were in a car accident. Granted, that's gonna look a little suspicious when no car is found, but I'll think of something. I'll explain that to you later. For now, Janella, we need to talk about your, uh, your powers."

"I do not understand."

"The way you slammed the door last night. Without touching it. It isn't—"

"Thomas? You home?" Eugenia's quick, light steps followed her voice up the stairs. Then she poked her perfectly made-up face through the bedroom door. "There you are. How's our patient this morning? Are you feeling better, hon?" She came right to the bed and perched on its opposite side. Gripping Janella's good hand in hers, she smiled. "Does it hurt much?"

Janella studied the pretty face. "Yes." The woman's hand was warm and soft on hers. Her face and voice were pleasant, and there was no threatening air about her. Janella shot Thomas a glance. "Thomas helped me."

"Well, sure he did. And I'm gonna help you, too. Has anyone called your family yet?"

Janella averted her face, trying not to show a hint of sadness. If this Eugenia saw it, she might assume Janella was weak and of little consequence. She might try to use that weakness against her, perhaps even try to steal Thomas away from her. Well, Janella thought, stiffening her shoulders, the woman would get a surprise if she put that theory to the test.

Janella sat straighter and kept her voice cool. "I have no family."

Eugenia's eyes widened. Then she was leaning over, her arm sliding around Janella's shoulders, gently cradling her head. "I didn't know. I'm sorry, hon. But surely there must be someone we can—"

"No. There is no one."

"Janella is on her own, 'Genia. She was just passing through last night, and—"

"Well, she's not on her own anymore." Eugenia straightened, and Janella saw a gleam of determination in her eyes, but no hint of malicious intent. She clasped Janella's hand in both of hers and looked right into her eyes. "You've got someone now, hon. You've got me. And Thomas, too. Sumac is a wonderful town. You're gonna like it here—you just wait and see."

Janella smiled, a little of the wariness leaving her. This woman practically bubbled over with uncensored emotions, unlike Thomas. Obviously she was the one of no consequence and of little strength. Either that, or things truly were different here. Just as her father had told her. Now that she saw Eugenia was no threat, Janella felt a bit more comfortable with her. "You are very kind."

Eugenia stood and pointed at the tray. "You eat your breakfast now, Janella. Such a pretty name, isn't it, Thomas? When can she get up and around, anyway? I can get the spare bedroom all ready for her, and—"

"You can stop right there, Eugenia. She's staying here."

Janella blinked at the censure in Thomas's voice. He was quite firm with this Eugenia. Would she put up with that? Janella was still certain she wanted him for her own, but he would need a lot of lessons in deferring to feminine authority. The man seemed to have no respect for his superiors.

Eugenia tilted her coppery crowned head, studying him. Then she looked at Janella again. "Well, Thomas Allan Duffy, can it be your stone heart's finally softening up?" Her brows rose and she nodded thoughtfully.

"Don't start with that crap, will you? I just want her where I can keep an eye on her... for the time being, anyway."

Eugenia frowned. "For the time being, then. But Thomas, you know how it will look. People will talk. As soon as she's able, she ought to come and stay with me."

Janella felt her eyes widen, but she fought not to let her touch of panic show in them. He could be as haughty and cold as he wanted, but Thomas was the only person she knew here. The only one she trusted. Male or otherwise. She most certainly wasn't going to leave him to go off with this stranger. And it would be silly to leave him, anyway, since he was going to be hers very soon.

He touched her shoulder, sent her a speaking look that seemed to tell her not to worry. It was the first hint of feeling she'd glimpsed in his hard eyes.

Staring hard at Eugenia, he said, "Since when have I given a damn if people talk?"

Eugenia shrugged. "*She* might care about her reputation, even if you don't," she said. "Meantime, Janella, is there anything you need?"

Janella thought for a minute. Then nodded. "I need a dog, I think."

Thomas blinked. Eugenia's brows lifted in surprise. "A dog?"

"Not to eat," she assured them quickly, thinking that might be the cause of their surprise. "Thomas says your people keep them as friends. I would like a big one as my friend. Bigger than Hum-phrey. Big enough to bite Humphrey's head off if he makes those loud noises at me again." She nodded, sending a smug glance at Thomas to tell him she'd prevail over this dog issue, one way or another. Once explained, they must see that her request made perfect sense.

Eugenia looked at Thomas. Thomas shrugged. "The head injury. She's still a little...disoriented."

"Oh." Eugenia reached down and patted Janella's hand. "Don't you worry about Humphrey, hon. He wouldn't hurt a fly." She smiled and sighed. "Wish I could stay, but I have to open up the shop. I'll check on you later, though."

Eugenia turned toward the door, and Thomas rose to walk her out.

"You left your container," Janella said. The small article the woman had carried was still on the bed at Janella's side. She sent it to Eugenia. Thomas turned first, his eyes widening as Eugenia's bag rose from the bed and moved toward her. He lunged as Eugenia turned, snatching the bag in midair. Janella frowned, wondering why he'd done that.

He held the bag out to Eugenia as Janella calmly picked up another orange wedge.

Eugenia frowned, but took it from him. "Thank you. I'd forget my head if it wasn't screwed on. Tootleloo, Janella."

"Tootleloo?" Janella frowned at the fruit in her hand. "I thought it was called orange?"

Eugenia blinked and her smile wavered. "Are you sure she doesn't need a hospital?" she whispered as Thomas took her elbow and escorted her out of the bedroom.

"Questioning my medical opinion, Eugenia?"

Janella heard no more. They moved into the hallway, and she concentrated on eating her breakfast.

He walked beside Eugenia down the stairs. As they moved through the kitchen, she paused at the table, pointing.

"There's a fresh coffee cake in the fridge, and I brought the morning paper in for you. Oddest things going on last night, Thomas. Reminds me of that time about thirty years ago or so...." She shook her head. "Ah, but listen to me rattling on. I have to get on into town. Haven't been late opening the shop since I retired from teaching. Wouldn't want to start now. You just call if you need anything."

She hurried out the door. Her '89 Cadillac roared like a frustrated bull as it shot out the driveway, spitting gravel in its wake.

Thomas stood in the doorway until she was out of sight. Humphrey nudged him hard, apparently disliking being ignored. Thomas scratched his head and Humphrey whined and bunted the screen door. "Yeah, okay, go on outside for awhile." Thomas pushed it open and Humphrey bounded out. Then he closed the door and shook his head slowly. This was not going to be easy. He passed the table on his way back through the kitchen and automatically grabbed the paper. His gaze caught one corner of the two-inch headline and he froze at the three letters he saw there.

He unfolded the paper and stared down at it, swearing under his breath. Hundreds Report UFO Over Sumac.

"Ah, damn..."

What's the big deal, he asked himself as he sat down and began scanning the article. Hell, it had made the papers before, too, but no one had really believed it.

Someone did.

Thomas groaned at that young voice invading his psyche yet again. He tried to ignore it, but the persistent little brat kept after him.

You know someone did. Those men in the dark suits who showed up the next day, asking questions around town. They even came to school. Remember?

Yeah, he remembered. He hadn't known what to make of the "men-in-black" at the time. He'd read since that, whoever they were, they showed up with some regularity in towns where UFO sightings were reported. Seemed the alien watchers had formed some kind of group. Had their own magazines, complete with blurred photos of what looked like Frisbees or hats tossed into the air and snapped "in flight." According to most of those members, the men-in-black— or MIB—were alien agents trying to keep witnesses silent. Thomas figured they were more likely government or military types.

Whoever they were, they could be a threat to Janella if they found out about her.

Thomas smirked and shook his head. "Right. Now, get real. They wouldn't believe me about Janella if I told them."

He dropped the paper when he heard her scream. Sprinting up the stairs with his heart trying to pound a hole through his rib cage, he battled nightmare images of her convulsing in reaction to something she'd eaten. He flung the bedroom door open so hard it crashed into the wall, but she wasn't in the rumpled bed.

The bathroom. The door was open, and he ran through it, then skidded to a stop. She stood in the shower stall, T-shirt and leggings still in place, dripping wet, coughing and spluttering and reaching blindly for the knobs to turn the cold water off.

He couldn't help it. He burst out laughing, even as he leaned over to twist the knob and stop the flow.

"It is not funny!" She pushed dark, dripping straggles off her face, rubbed water from her eyes.

"Oh, yeah, it is, Janella. It's funnier than hell."

She glared at him. "You . . . you dog! I only wanted to see what the dial controlled."

He laughed a little harder, but managed to grab a towel from the shelf and hold it out to her. She didn't take it, nor did she stop glaring at him.

He flung the towel at her, leaving her little choice but to catch it. She muttered as she wiped the water from her face and neck, and began rubbing her hair.

"No man laughs at Janella," she stated flatly.

"This one does," he returned. She was an arrogant little thing—he could say that much. It was good that her attitude rubbed him the wrong way. It would help him stay aloof. He refused to think about just how long it had been since anything had made him laugh out loud. Instead, he glanced downward once, and regretted it instantly. He suddenly understood the popularity of those infamous wet T-shirt contests. The soaked, all-but-transparent material molded to her like a second skin. The shapes of her full, round breasts, chilled peaks and all, were as fully revealed as they would be were she stark naked. Which was just as well, since she angrily stripped the shirt over her head and began rubbing herself vigorously.

Thomas wouldn't have been human if he hadn't looked just a little. But he quickly ordered his eyes to focus elsewhere, and turned his back.

"That's what we call a shower. It's got hot water as well as cold. It's for bathing." He heard her slipping the tight-fitting pants off, stepping out of them.

"I wish you had told me sooner." She tapped his shoulder and he turned slightly. "I've covered myself. You will not burn your eyes out if you look at me."

Seemed to irritate her that he wouldn't gawk at her naked. Well, he couldn't help it. It was tough enough looking at her with clothes on. He turned around, smiling in spite of himself at the awkward way she held the towel against her.

"Come on, I'll find you something to wear. Then we'll check to see just how thoroughly you ruined the cast." He returned to his bedroom, yanked open a drawer and managed to dig out a pair of shorts with an elastic waist and another T-shirt. He handed them to her. "I'll get you some better things today. Shouldn't be too much of a problem. Eugenia owns a clothing store in town."

She took the clothes from him, and when he saw the towel slipping away he quickly turned his back again. What, did the women up on Krypton run around naked all the time? She certainly acted it.

"You are kind to me," she told him, as she dressed. And it sounded as if she hated having to say it. As if every word were being forced through grated teeth. But maybe she was through being angry with him for laughing. "I hope you will not expect me to go to the woman Eugenia. I want to stay with you."

It was half heartfelt admission, half command. But there had been no kind of request to her words. As if she didn't expect him to refuse her. He would have liked to disagree, just to show her who was in charge around here, but he'd already decided she'd be better off with him. Still, just agreeing with her was a little too much to ask of him.

"Well, it's a good thing. 'Cause you're staying here whether you like it or not."

Her brows drew together, chin coming up a little higher. "I'll stay here with you because it is what I want."

He turned, ready to do battle. Who the hell did she think she was, anyway?

But the sight of her in his baggy shorts dissolved his irritation with her. He damned near laughed again. Then his amusement died when a hairbrush rose from the dresser and floated right into her waiting hand.

"Will she be angry that I refuse her offer?"

"No, she'll be fine." It still gave him the willies to see her do that. "Janella, I need to point something out to you."

She faced him, continuing to brush her hair and waiting for him to speak.

"You know the way you just made that hairbrush come to you, without actually touching it?"

She tilted her head to one side, frowning.

"We can't do that."

"I do not understand."

"Okay, say I want that book over there." He pointed to the Louis L'Amour paperback on the dresser. "The only way I can get it is to walk over there, put my hands on it and pick it up."

Her brows rose in fine arches. "You cannot bring it to you?"

"Nope."

"How bothersome that must be!"

He closed his eyes for a second, opened them again. "The point is, Janella, that if you go around moving things without touching them, people are going to know you're different. You want to keep your little secret, you're gonna have to try to remember not to do that."

She nodded slowly. "Yes. I see. It will not be easy, Thomas. I've been moving things that way since I was born. I do it without really thinking first."

"Yeah, well, if you do it around here, it's going to lead to trouble."

She nodded. "I will try. There is so much to remember. Keep my breasts covered, do not move things, dogs are not for meat." She rolled her eyes.

He chewed his inner cheek and wished she'd turn bitchy again so he could try to remember how to dislike her. "How are you feeling?" As he spoke, he moved closer, took the plaster-heavy arm in his hands and tested the dampness. It wasn't too bad. She'd had sense enough to hold it out away from the spray.

"Much better than before, Thomas." She glanced down at the cast as he ran his hands over it. "But this is heavy and uncomfortable. How long will it stay?"

"Six weeks."

She closed her eyes, counted on her fingers. "Six... That is forty-two of your days, Thomas!"

He nodded. "'Fraid so."

"But a bone takes only two of your days to heal. Why must I wear it so long?"

Thomas blinked in shock. "A bone takes..." He shook his head. "Ours take six weeks. Maybe you heal faster. Tell you what, after two days we'll have it x-rayed, and..." He sighed hard, pushing a hand through his hair. "Damn, I can't do that, either. A mild dose of radiation might kill you." He frowned and thought about it. "We can take the cast off and see how the arm feels, how much use you have. That ought to tell us all we need to know."

"I could heal in an hour at home by injecting a drug that reconstructs the cells. But not here. I will simply have to wait, as you suggest."

He tilted his head to one side, studying her. "You gave up a lot coming here. Your planet must be light-years ahead of us technologically."

She licked her lips, nodded. "There is more to life than technology, Thomas."

He wanted to ask what the drug was, how it was developed and whether it could be duplicated on Earth. But all of that fled his mind at the intense sadness that glimmered in her eyes all of the sudden. Hell, he could almost feel her throat closing up, the burning behind her eyes, the tightness in her chest. When she bit her lip, averting her face and blinking her eyes dry, he realized his arms were moving, rising, reaching toward her. He slammed them down to his sides, balled fists probably bruising his own thighs.

"So, other than the arm, how do you feel?"

"Fine. The pain is less now than last night. I imagine it will not hurt at all by the end of the day."

Her voice was a little rougher than normal, softer. Damn, what had she been thinking about that made her so sad? What the hell had she run away from?

"I need to go into town. I work there, at the clinic. You remember, I told you I was a doctor."

"Doctor." She faced him again, shocking him with the sudden transformation. Her smile damn near blinded him, and her still-damp eyes gleamed. "Healer. You are needed in this...*clinic*...to heal your people?"

"Yes."

She closed her eyes slowly. "You do this every day?"

He tilted his head, knowing she was curious about everything, but still a little thrown by the emotion in her eyes. It made him decidedly uncomfortable. "I take weekends off, unless there's an emergency. Thing is, you can't stay here alone. You ought to come along with me. I'm just wondering if you're up to it."

She lifted her chin a little higher, put her good hand on her hip and struck a stance. "I am strong, Thomas. As strong as you." Her gaze lowered to his upper arms, narrowed. "Well, nearly as strong. And I want to come with you, to watch you heal them. More than that, I want to help you. Will you teach me how?"

For crying out loud! Would wonders never cease? He studied her and shook his head. "It'll take more than one day in the clinic to teach you anything."

Her lower lip pushed out just a little, and she looked so disappointed he had to swallow another healthy dose of surprise. "But I suppose you could help some. As long as you feel well enough."

"Yes!"

He nodded, studying her, wondering. "What did you do back there, Janella?"

Her lips thinned a little. That proud chin lowered. "I was in training."

"Training for what?"

She sighed, not meeting his eyes. "To take my place in the ruling house."

Thomas frowned. It sounded like something she ought to be proud of. But she didn't seem proud. It might explain her attitude, though. Maybe she was used to having her every command obeyed. "So, why'd you leave?"

She met his eyes, hers dark and distant. "I couldn't stay."

It was all she was going to say, he sensed. She didn't feel comfortable enough with him yet to tell him her most troubling secrets. Okay, he could wait.

Damn! What the hell was he thinking? He didn't *want* to know her secrets, didn't care one ounce what caused the sadness he saw lurking like a shadow on her soul. And he wasn't going to.

Turning away from her, he busied himself digging into the dresser for some clean clothes. "I'll just shower and then we'll be on our way," he told her.

Chapter 4

He put her into a primitive vehicle that bounded and growled over bumpy paths, amid beautiful lands. She couldn't take her gaze from the scene outside the noisy vehicle. Wide, vivid green fields, and golden ones, their crops swaying like a dance with every touch of the breeze. All beneath a sky so blue and cloudless it nearly brought tears to her eyes. So different here. At home the crops were grown in special buildings, without benefit of natural soil. Only chemical mineral solutions and artificial sunlight. And with the population problem, there were no more open spaces like this. Just cities, sterile immaculate cities, everywhere. And the only animals were those on display in a few scattered facilities. Trapped behind fences with manmade rocks and streams, fake trees and grass.

His vehicle bumped along onto a paved path, between neat rows of small buildings. Sumac Feed and

Grain, she read, and inhaled the sweet scents coming from the place. Sumac Farm Supply. Sumac John Deere, whatever that was. Sumac Health Center.

"There's a combination grocery store, pharmacy and gas station a little farther on this road. The post office and a used-car dealership are down that road on the right. Across from those there's a restaurant, a hardware store and a bar. And that's about it."

She didn't know what he meant by all those things, but she would learn. He pulled the vehicle to a stop in front of a small brick building, which had been painted garishly pink. The sign above the door read The Pink Petunia, and had a flower surrounding the words. In the big front window forms stood, probably to display the clothing the forms wore.

He got out first, then came around and opened her door. She smiled, glad to see he was finally showing some deference to her gender. He took her hand and led her inside, again holding the door for her. Some of the people passing by turned to stare openly at her, and Janella squirmed a bit, wondering what they were thinking.

"Well, look who's come to call." Eugenia eyed Janella, the clothes she wore. "Oh, my, no wonder I'm your first stop."

There were others in the shop, as well. An older woman, who peered curiously over her antiquated eyeglasses. A young, attractive one, who watched Janella with raised brows. A teenager who wore paint on her face and ornaments in her ears.

"Well, come on, hon, we've got no time to lose." Janella only stared at Thomas as Eugenia took her by the hand. "You can go on to the clinic, Thomas,"

Eugenia told him. "I'll bring her over when we finish up here."

Janella stiffened, not wanting to be left alone here with these strangers. Fear twisted to life in her stomach, and she shot Thomas a pleading look.

He met her gaze, then glanced down at the band around his wrist. "I've still got some time before my first appointment. Think I'll hang around."

Relief flooded her, and Janella sighed with it. Eugenia only looked from her to Thomas and back again, then shrugged and led her into a back room.

Then, one by one, Eugenia brought articles of clothing for her to try on. The tops and bottoms—she called them jeans—were self-evident, but the torturous-looking white scraps of material that could only be made to harness the breasts were ludicrous. Janella refused even to consider them. There were pretty things, though. Soft, lacy undergarments, and blouses of something she called silk. The jeans were comfortable, and she liked them at once. She kept a pair of them on, along with a silk blouse of vivid green.

It took over an hour to choose, and when she finished, she paused a moment to consider that this primitive culture likely still used some form of currency. She had none, didn't even know what value might be placed on the clothing Eugenia was packing into bags right now. She stepped into the front room again to ask about it, when she saw Thomas hand the woman several green-colored slips of paper.

Eugenia took only a portion and gave him back the rest. "You handle half, Thomas, and I'll eat the other half. It's the least I can do." She winked at him and smiled.

"Not thinking of adopting her like you do every stray thing that comes along, are you, Eugenia?"

She shrugged. "What's the harm? Unless you plan to keep her all to yourself?"

"Dream on, lady."

Janella frowned, wondering again if this female planned to choose Thomas as her mate. In fact, several females in the store seemed to be looking at him with some degree of speculation in their eyes. Janella found she did not like the idea. In fact, she hated it. No doubt any wife of his would make it her first order of business to sweep Janella out of her household like unwanted dust. And that just wouldn't do.

Besides, she thought as she studied him from behind, she had decided to keep him for herself. She'd known he would be hers almost from the day she'd met him so long ago. And despite his coolness toward her, she hadn't changed her mind. He had as many good qualities as bad. He'd have to learn to take orders a bit better, but all in all, he wouldn't make a bad mate. He was certainly nice enough to look at, and Janella imagined coupling with him would be extremely pleasant.

She stood closer to him and slipped her arm through his as a broad hint the other women couldn't help but take. She doubted any of them would be willing to fight for the right to claim him. But if they did, then Janella was more than up for the challenge.

When he turned and looked at her in those tight-fitting jeans, with the thin silk whispering over her breasts and no bra underneath, Thomas almost choked. And when she stood so close, her body pressed to his from thigh to shoulder, and gripped his arm, he felt himself squirm. Every woman in that shop was gawking, and he knew damned well the whole town would start speculating about her before the day was out. What the hell was she up to, clinging to his arm like that?

He sidled away from her, scooped up the packages and carried them out the door, feeling too many female eyes on his back as he left. 'Lisbeth Crabtree had been in there. And God knows there wasn't a bigger gossip in Sumac than 'Lisbeth. Besides which, she'd been actively trying to rope and brand him for one of four daughters. He didn't think she much cared which one, either.

He loaded the back of the Jeep with the things she'd bought and left it parked where it was, in the small square lot in front of The Pink Petunia. Taking Janella's hand, he led her across the road to the clinic.

Opening the door with a flourish, he held it for her and she went in before him.

"This is where I work."

"Where you heal," she said, nodding. Her gaze scanned the carpeted room, the rack of magazines and the chairs lining the walls. She walked over to the toy box and peeked inside, glanced up at the television mounted on a pole in the corner.

"This is a waiting room, Janella. I can only see one person at a time. The others sit here and wait their turn." He pointed to the desk, on the other side of a partition. "And this is Rosa, my receptionist. Rosa, meet Janella...uh, Smith. She's going to be working with us for a while."

Rosa stood, eyeing Janella curiously, muttering a rather unwelcoming hello. He glanced at Janella and saw a distasteful look on her face. The two seemed to be sizing each other up like a couple of boxers in opposite corners of a ring, waiting for the bell.

"Working with us?" Rosa glanced back at him, dark brows lifted, brown eyes more than curious.

"That's right. She's a friend of mine, visiting from out of town. I've been telling her what a *friendly* little town we have here."

Rosa's lips thinned a little. "Doing what?"

Seemed she was choosing to ignore his hint.

"Assisting me with patients."

"She's a nurse?"

"Is there any coffee made, Rosa?" He was damned if he'd put up with the third degree from an employee.

Rosa turned to the fresh pot on the counter behind her, poured him a cup and handed it to him. She glanced at Janella. "Feel free to help yourself."

Janella's glare heated a bit. "I do not like coffee."

Thomas sighed hard. "Come on, Janella. I'll show you around."

As they walked past her, Rosa went to the desk, pulled the chair out and started to sit. Thomas saw the mischievous gleam in Janella's eyes just before the chair suddenly scooted a foot backward. Rosa was on the floor, spitting mad, before he could even shout a warning. And Janella smiled with contentment.

He pulled her into the first treatment room they came to and closed the door. "Dammit Janella, just what the hell do you think you're doing?"

She blinked up at him, ebony eyes all innocence.

"You moved that chair, didn't you?"

She bit her lip, but it didn't prevent her contented smile. "She made me angry."

"That's no excuse."

A little frown appeared between her brows. "I wasn't aware I needed an excuse."

Thomas closed his eyes, praying for mercy. Just what the hell had he gotten himself into? He gripped Janella's shoulders for emphasis. "Don't *ever* do *anything* like that again. Understand?"

"Thomas? Are *you* telling *me* what to do? Giving *me* an order?"

"Damn straight, I am. You might have been some kind of despot-in-training back in Nowhere Land, but here, you're no better than anybody else."

"But I'm a *woman!*"

"So what? You want a medal?"

She blinked as if in shock.

Thomas shook his head, trying to stay angry with her. He knew damned well, though, that Rosa had been just as rude as was humanly possible, and probably deserved what she got. And there was part of him that wanted to laugh out loud about it. That part that never took any crap from anybody. He couldn't help but admire Janella's spunk. Not only that, but when her eyes sparkled with mischief they damn near blinded him.

And now they were clouded and puzzled and she looked like that lost, frightened little girl again. Hell, how was he going to keep the cold, unemotional moat he'd built around himself intact with someone like Janella? Especially if he kept noticing those almond-shaped eyes, and the feelings they expressed so plainly.

Wasn't it bad enough that his body was rapidly developing a strong hankering to get to know hers... intimately? Did he have to *like* the damned woman, as well?

Sighing, he yanked the door open. "Rosa, bring me the file on the Meyers kid. And call Saint Luke's for a report on Hugh Connor, will you?"

When Rosa arrived with the file folder, Thomas knew Janella was staring. Her eyes registered something between confusion and disbelief. Rosa left to make the call, and Thomas closed the door again.

"What's the matter now?"

Janella only shook her head, blinking. "She... she *obeyed* you."

The way she'd said the word "obeyed" made it sound like something obscene. "She works for me, Janella. I pay her to *obey* me."

There wasn't time to delve into whatever was making her look so thunderstruck. The first patient arrived, and Rosa led mother and son into the room.

Eugenia didn't like the looks of the three strangers who waltzed into the shop. Not one bit. City folks, she could tell at a glance. They wore nearly identical dark-colored suits, and long black coats that were too heavy for early autumn.

Still, she pasted a smile on her face and set her paperback on the counter. "What can I do for you gentlemen? You lost?"

Only the tall blond one came forward, leaving the other two lingering behind him like shadows. His smile was toothy, big and, she thought, probably false. He was handsome. Dangerously so.

He thrust a hand at her. She shook it, just to be polite. "I'm Jack Halloway, ma'am. I'm with the U.S. Air Force."

She lifted her brows. "Oh, yeah? Where's your uniform?"

He smiled again. "Don't wear them in my line of work. Are you Ms. Overton?"

She nodded, feeling more uneasy by the second. The bell over the door jangled. Sylvie Grayson peeked in, frowned hard and backed right out again.

"Maybe you ought to tell me what you want and be on your way, Mr. Halloway. You're scaring off my customers."

He nodded a little sheepishly. "We're investigating that reported UFO sighting. You must have seen it in this morning's paper."

She nodded, wary. "Didn't see any UFO, though. Don't tell me my tax dollars pay you guys to chase flying saucers around Iowa."

"Now, Ms. Overton, no one said anything about a flying saucer."

Eugenia tilted her head. "Some government test thing, wasn't it? Lord, I hope you nuts haven't decided to use Sumac skies to try out some nuclear-powered war machine. This is a farming town, mister. We don't need your experiments crashing in our woods, spreading whatever kinds of contaminants that power 'em into our water supply."

His brows went up. "You don't have to worry about that. I'm here to prevent any such thing from happening." He laid a well-manicured hand on the counter. "Now, you say something crashed in the woods?"

"I didn't say that."

"You alluded to it." He pinned her with his pale-blue gaze. "Come on, Ms. Overton. Why don't you tell me what you saw?"

"Well...I, it's just that I..." She felt trapped. She wasn't sure she should tell him about that funny glow that had briefly lit up the night sky out toward Thomas's place. He sure wouldn't want these men poking around over there. Besides, that flash of light was caused by Janella's car accident. Wasn't it?

"What did you see, Ms. Overton?"

A form stopped outside, drawing Eugenia's gaze. A tall man stood there, near the display window. She blinked as she stared at his close-cropped sable beard peppered with white here and there and those warm sapphire eyes. He looked at her, right at her, with those eyes and gave his head a nearly imperceptible shake.

"Ms. Overton?" Halloway prompted.

She licked her lips nervously, tugging her gaze free of the grip the newcomers had on it. What in the world was going on here? Who were all these strangers, anyway?

Stiffening her spine, she made herself answer him. "I didn't see anything, Mr. Halloway. Not a thing. And I really don't think anyone else did, either. Sumac's a nice town, but it can get kind of dull for some tastes. We have a few overactive imaginations around just to keep things interesting."

The bearded man gave her a heart-stopping smile, and then he winked. Eugenia caught her breath as he walked out of sight.

"You sure about that?" Halloway was asking.

"What? Oh, yes, of course I'm sure. I'd certainly remember if I'd seen a UFO, now, wouldn't I?"

Janella battled tears all day as she watched Thomas work. She didn't do much other than hand him things, quickly learning the names of various tools and medicines and bandages. But her emotions kept her from thinking as clearly as she might have been able to do. There had been an elderly man with a heart condition, who'd regaled her with one funny story after another as Thomas examined him. Then a little girl in a wheelchair, who'd gazed up at him with trusting eyes as he worked. And later, the sweetest six-year-old boy with what Thomas called Down's syndrome. He'd been nervous, and Janella had held his hand throughout his visit. Before the boy left, he'd hugged her neck and planted a wet kiss on her cheek. That was when her tears finally spilled over. She averted her face in time to hide them from the boy and his mother, but not from Thomas.

He frowned at her after they'd gone. "What's wrong?"

She shook her head, brushing her face dry with the back of one hand. She couldn't tell him that at home, none of those people would have been given a chance at survival. No one there would care for them the way Thomas had done. If he knew, he'd probably think her as barbaric and cold as the rest of her people. But she wasn't. And for so long, she'd wondered if she was weak, somehow flawed because of her feelings.

Seeing him with those special, wonderful people today had proved to her that she'd been right all along. It wasn't she who was flawed; it was the society she'd been born into. She only wished she could make them see it.

"Janella?"

She bit her lip. "Nothing is wrong, Thomas. I am just...just very happy to be here." She couldn't stop looking at him and thinking that she'd never in her life known a man like him. "You're a special man, Thomas. A good man."

The concern left his face then. He appeared wary, instead. "Not really."

"Yes, you are. The way you care for these people, it—"

"No, Janella. Don't get confused about it. I don't care for them. I just take care of them."

She frowned. "I don't understand."

Thomas lowered his head, his breath escaping in a rush. "First rule of medicine, Janella. Keep an emotional distance. It's necessary." His voice a little softer, he added, "Believe me, I *know.*"

Janella tried to see his meaning in his eyes, but they were carefully blank, as they had been for most of the day. In fact, now that she thought about it, she realized that *he* hadn't held the little boy's hand or hugged him. He hadn't laughed at any of the old man's stories. He'd just gone about his examination, almost pretending not to hear them.

"Emotional distance" was the term he'd used. But in the time she'd known him, she hadn't seen him show much emotion at all. Except when he'd laughed at her in the shower.

It was so confusing. Why would a man spend his life helping people unless he cared? And if he didn't care, then was he just like the people she'd left behind? Unfeeling? Cold?

Somehow she just couldn't believe that. She decided to watch him more closely from now on. Maybe she'd figure it out. Maybe she'd figure a lot of things out. Like why he didn't seem to have any deference to women, and why Rosa had rushed all day to obey his every request. This Earth was a puzzling place.

Chapter 5

She watched television with an intensity that would have been laughable. Except that she kept looking at him with the same studious, curious expression every few seconds. And he got the sneaking suspicion she was comparing him with the men she saw on the screen, and he wouldn't have been human if he hadn't wondered how he measured up. Not that he cared.

The movie was *Casablanca*. When it ended, she was blinking away tears. Thomas smiled a little. Seemed he had a softhearted little alien on his hands.

"Did you like the movie?"

She nodded hard, brushing her cheeks dry with one hand. "It was wonderful, but so sad."

Thomas thumbed the rewind button on the VCR. She was staring at him again. Her almond-shaped eyes narrow, probing. "I think I understand better now."

"Understand what?"

She only shrugged, rose from the sofa and went to the shelf that was lined with videocassettes. Humphrey lay in her path, oblivious to the world. She skirted him warily. He lifted his head, eyeing her, watching her every move. The two didn't much like each other, but Thomas thought Humphrey had gotten over his initial hostility. Now he was only suspicious and watchful.

Janella studied the tapes. "Can we watch another?"

"Sure. Watch them all night if you want. Best way I can think of to learn about life on Earth. Just don't take them too literally, Janella. Reality is a lot more mundane than the movies."

"I don't know about that," she said softly, not looking at him, pulling out one tape after another. "Rick seemed a good example of human behavior."

Thomas shifted on the couch, trying not to focus solely on her perfect bottom filling out those jeans. And failing. "In what way?"

"He appeared cold at first. Unfeeling, without emotion. But it was only his way of protecting himself from being hurt again." She decided on a tape and turned toward him, holding it in her hand. "It makes sense, don't you think? I would think that might be a common reaction to pain."

He pursed his lips, nodded. "I guess it might be. I don't know, I'm not a psychologist."

She smiled, lifting the tape. "What is this one about?"

He grinned at her selection. Disney's *Beauty and the Beast*. "It's a children's movie. But you'll probably like it." He got up, ejected the tape that was in the VCR and took the one she held.

"Why do you have children's movies, Thomas? You have no children."

He shrugged, fast-forwarding through the previews. "No, but I have a lot of young patients. They get bored when they have to stay in the hospital for any length of time, so I buy videos and take them in. Keeps their minds off their medical problems."

She didn't comment, and when he glanced her way it was to see the most smug, knowing expression in her eyes. Almost an I-told-you-so sort of a look, but he couldn't imagine why.

Giving the dog a wide berth, she returned to her seat on the sofa. Humphrey only lowered his head again when she was sitting still. The opening music played, and Thomas sat beside her. He reached into the bowl on the coffee table for a handful of potato chips. Humphrey lifted his head and emitted a soft "Woof."

Janella stiffened.

"He's talking to me," Thomas told her.

She blinked twice, glanced from him to the dog and back again. "What is he saying?"

"He wants a potato chip. He loves the things. Here." Thomas took her hand in his, turned it palm up and placed a chip in it. "Why don't you give it to him?"

"He'll bite my hand off. He hates me." Her eyes widened as Humphrey got to his feet and planted himself in front of her, waiting with his tail wagging a mile a minute. "Make him sit down, Thomas. I cannot see the movie."

"Oh, he won't sit down until he gets a chip. And I'm not going to give him one."

She glared at him, but he only nodded toward the dog. "Go on, try it. I promise, he won't hurt you. You trust me, don't you?"

She nodded, warily, and shifted the chip to her fingertips. Slowly she held her hand out to the dog. Humphrey leaned forward and took it. He crunched it down with relish, staring at Janella. She stared back. Humphrey sighed contentedly, turned around three times and lay down right on top of Janella's feet. She tilted her head, staring down at him as if puzzled.

"You see?" Thomas asked. "Now he's your friend. You gave him his favorite treat and he's grateful."

Biting her lip, Janella reached a wary hand downward and very timidly stroked the dog's head. Humphrey closed his eyes and sighed more loudly than before. She smiled softly, settled back on the sofa, a little closer to Thomas than she'd been before. He tried to focus on the movie, instead of on the way it felt to be sitting in a darkened room with her this way. Sort of intimate, and extremely uncomfortable. The pendant he wore felt warm against his skin.

Janella glanced at the glass of cola on the table, and it levitated, then floated into her waiting hand. She took a sip and returned it in the same manner.

Long after Thomas had gone to his bed, Janella stayed up watching movies. And with every one, she felt she understood a bit more about these people and their ways. Thomas had explained how to operate the VCR before going up, so she could study to her heart's content.

And the revelations were enlightening. The most important of all was that it seemed women were not the rulers of this planet. The males didn't obey them or serve them or even seem to fear them. Odd concept, but one she supposed she could adjust to. In fact, in some of the films, it appeared the women were the ones in subjugation. But in most, the sexes behaved almost as equals. Fascinating.

The other interesting difference was in the mating rituals of these people. Since neither sex was dominant, the choosing of a mate seemed to be a terribly complicated process, consisting of several steps. First, one recognized his or her attraction to the other. Then one agonized while trying to discern if the other felt the same, and went to great lengths to try to attract the other's attention. After that, one spent far too much time, in Janella's opinion, working up the courage to declare his or her feelings to the other. It was all very odd.

Janella had never once considered that she would have to do anything to attract the mate of her choice. At home, she would only have had to choose. It would have been an honor for any of the men to be picked and she couldn't imagine one who would object to it.

Here, things were going to be much more difficult. She realized with a little start that if she wanted Thomas as her own, she would first have to convince him that *he* wanted *her.*

It was such a ludicrous notion she blinked in shock.

And as she recalled the hostile glances of the women in the town, she knew there were plenty of others who'd like to claim him. Fighting for the right to claim him would do little good, for the choice was his.

Oh, dear, this was going to be a terrible effort. From all she'd seen on the screen tonight, there seemed to be an incredible amount of work involved. She would have to dress in satins and learn to apply the face paint as the women in the films did. She would have to learn to... oh, what was that word? Flirt. Yes, that was it. To flutter the eyelashes, and laugh softly, and make veiled, slightly suggestive comments, while making them seem unintentional.

She frowned at the sleeping dog and wriggled her toe from beneath his fur. Then she tiptoed past him, not quite as secure in his friendship now that Thomas had left the room, and inserted a fresh tape into the VCR. She was still confused about several things, and she would study these tapes until everything came clear in her mind.

Thomas found her there in the morning, still in yesterday's clothes, slumped sideways, sound asleep. From the stack of tapes on top of the VCR, it looked as if she'd been up most of the night. He stifled a laugh and moved quietly past her to put on a pot of coffee and see what he could find for breakfast.

When he turned from the sink, with a carafe of water, she was standing in the doorway, watching him.

"Sorry. I didn't mean to wake you. How'd the film festival go?"

She shrugged, scuffing to the table and sinking into a chair. "I enjoyed it very much. But I'm still confused."

Thomas poured the water into the coffeemaker, set the carafe underneath and turned it on. He refused to notice her tousled hair and sleep-hazy eyes. Or to let himself think that she looked almost as if she'd just been thoroughly made love to, instead of just having had a long night on the couch. In fact, he'd pretty much decided it was best not to think about sex at all when Janella was around. It tended to make his jeans too tight.

"I'm not surprised. What are you confused about, Janella? Maybe I can clear it up for you."

"Is it, or is it not acceptable to have sex before one is...um...married?"

Thomas felt his brows shoot up. "Sheesh, you cut to the chase, don't you?" He fished a pair of bowls and spoons from the dishwasher, dropped them on the table and reached into a cupboard for a box of cereal. If his hands were unsteady, it was just because he hadn't had a cup of coffee yet this morning. And he could and would answer what was a perfectly logical question, in a calm and professional manner.

"That's kind of complicated. I guess these days, it's pretty much a matter of personal choice. Some people consider it immoral, some don't." He grabbed the milk from the fridge and sat down across from her to fill his bowl.

"And what is your personal choice?"

Thomas sloshed milk onto the table. He steadied his hand, set the carton down and met her gaze. Damn. She was dead serious about this.

"That's a personal question, Janella. You can't just go around asking people about their sex lives." He reached for a napkin and mopped up his spill.

"I'm not asking just anyone. I'm asking you. How am I supposed to know how to act unless you explain things to me?"

He studied her, wondering just when she'd become so damned interested in knowing about Earth's moral standards concerning sex. "Why the sudden interest, Janella? You considering having sex with someone?"

She lowered her gaze quickly. "I was only curious." She reached for the box, filled her bowl carefully, just as he'd done, and then added milk.

Thomas licked his lips and tried telling himself this was not a wise conversation to be having with her. Not with her sitting there all rumpled, her wild hair tempting him to smooth it with his fingers, her eyes soft and sleepy.

"How did you handle sex back on Krypton?"

She scowled at his name for her planet, but still didn't meet his gaze. "It's forbidden until one's mate is chosen."

His throat went dry. "Did you... have a mate?"

She shook her head. "No. But I have often wondered what coupling would be like. Have you done it, Thomas?"

He almost groaned aloud, suddenly losing interest in his cereal. "Yeah."

"But not with a... a wife?"

Her jet eyes were on him now, searching his face, wide with curiosity.

"No, not with a wife."

"What is it like?"

He shoved his bowl away from him. "It's pleasant, okay? Can we change the subject now?"

"Did you love the woman, Thomas? Or did you do this only to relieve your physical needs?"

"For crying out loud—"

She jerked a little at his tone, eyes widening. "I've made you angry. I'm sorry, Thomas, I only wanted to know—"

"All right, all right. No, I didn't love any of them. Yes, it was only physical, and before you ask, the reason for that is that's the way I want it. That's the *only* way I want it. Now, will you please eat your cereal and get your butt upstairs to shower and dress? We have to be at the clinic by eight."

She stared at him for a long moment, and he could see the questions in her eyes. She wanted an explanation. But she didn't ask for one. Instead, she finally nodded and focused on her breakfast.

Maybe the movies hadn't been such a great idea after all. Films today were nothing but sex and violence anyway. Good thing he hadn't had a copy of *Rambo* lying around. She'd probably be asking for an Uzi.

Thomas sipped his coffee, glanced across at her, and saw the slightly wounded look she wore. Hell, he'd hurt her feelings, snapping at her that way. But how did she expect him to keep his distance when she sat there talking about sex as if she were thinking of trying it?

"You know, Janella, maybe you ought to read some books. They might give you a much clearer picture of things than the movies can."

She brightened, nodded hard. "Books. Yes, that's a good idea. I will . . . *I'll* do that."

In the Bear Road Café, three strangers in suits and ties sat at a corner booth, listening to the locals rattle on. So far no one had mentioned a UFO sighting. Seemed they were all up in arms over some local doctor's indiscretions. Still, you never knew what you might pick up on from casual conversation.

Jack Halloway chewed his bagel and pretended to read the morning paper, while the tape recorder in his coat pocket whirred almost silently.

"She's livin' with him!"

"What, all alone out there on the farm?"

"That's right. Pretty thing, too."

"Rosa's fit to be tied. Had her sights on the doc herself."

"So I heard. Rosa says she don't know what that girl is, but she's no nurse, that's for—"

"And goin' by the name of Smith. If that isn't the most unlikely—"

"You ladies ever do anything besides gossip?"

The one male voice in the room came from the gangly young man behind the counter. Skip, Halloway had heard him called. The others came from the table just behind his. All female, all married and, apparently, all very upset over the local doc's love life.

"Who do those city girls think they are, anyway? Waltzing in here like they were born and bred, and waltzing right back out again with *our* men."

"Yeah, but *what* city do you think this one's from? Rosa said she talks funny."

"I saw her at The Pink Petunia, hangin' on the doc's arm like she owned him. She was wearing a cast, too."

"Yup. Talk is she was in some kind of accident the other night. Doc Duffy found her and took her home with him."

One of them sniffed indignantly, as if to say taking her home had been the least he'd done with the woman. Halloway pulled a wallet out of his inner pocket. He'd pay up and leave. This was getting them nowhere.

"Musta been some accident. Did you see that light in the sky? Looked like a bomb went off."

Halloway went a little rigid in his seat, his gaze leaping up and meeting that of one of the men across from him. He forced himself to relax, replaced his wallet and took another bite of the bagel.

"I saw it. That couldn't have been her, though. That flash came from the woods out back of Duffy's place. No roads out there."

"Some kind of government test, I bet. And what do those loonies at the paper do but call it a UFO! Hey, Skip, a little more coffee over here."

"Yeah, I'm coming."

"Well, what I saw that night sure looked like nothing I've seen before. Just a green streak, crossing the sky, and then that white flash. Scared my socks off, I can tell you."

"What doesn't, Agnes? You get scared over every thunderstorm."

"It was no UFO. Likely one of those satellites they got floatin' around overhead just petered out and came down. Don't know what everyone's getting so fired up about."

"You don't suppose that foreign city woman will lure the doc back to wherever she came from, do you?"

"Wouldn't be surprised. And where would we be then?"

"I just wish Rosa would hog-tie that man and marry him."

"Rosa! He's not interested in Rosa. Now, if he'd just take a second glance at my Becky, I know he'd—"

"Aw, 'Lisbeth, you've done everything but shackle the man to Becky Jo, and he hasn't so much as blinked."

Jack Halloway nodded to his two counterparts, rose and walked to the register to pay for their breakfasts. As he handed the man his money, he smiled his friendliest smile. "Say...Skip, isn't it? You couldn't tell me where I might find a Dr. Duffy, could you?"

The man at the register looked Halloway up and down, then nodded. "This time of day, he'd be at the clinic. Back the way you came and turn left. Can't miss it."

"Thanks, but I didn't want to see him at the clinic. I was talking about his farm."

The man frowned. "You a friend of his?"

Halloway nodded. "Yeah, and I've come a long way to see him. Can you help me out?"

In a corner booth near the windows, a tall man sat, absently rubbing his salt-and-pepper beard and listening.

Janella glanced out through the display window of The Pink Petunia for the fortieth time and emitted a sigh.

"He's only been gone an hour, hon." Eugenia patted her hand and smiled. "He'll be back soon."

Janella blinked, a little startled that she'd been so obvious. Thomas had asked her to stay here while he went to the hospital to check on a patient. He hadn't wanted her there because, he said, she might inadvertently be exposed to some illness or other, one against which her body might have no resistance. It made sense. But Janella didn't like it.

"You're sweet on him, aren't you?"

Janella blinked, then frowned. "What do you mean?"

"Thomas. You like him, don't you?" Eugenia filled Janella's teacup as she spoke, then added more steaming liquid to her own.

"Of course I like him." Janella took a sip. She really liked the fragrant tea. Much nicer than that bitter swill Thomas called coffee. "He's been very good to me."

"Come on, Janella. You can tell me." Eugenia winked at her.

"Tell you what?"

Eugenia's lips pursed, and she sighed. "Oh, fine. Be as coy as you want. Just remember, I'm on your side."

"On my side?"

"Yes." She looked down, shook her head slowly. "You know, he used to be so different. Happy and easygoing. Since he came back, he's a different man. Stiff as a board, and so cold it gives most people goose bumps. But he hasn't changed inside, Janella. I think maybe his heart's just taken an extended nap. All he needs is a good woman to shake him right from his head to his toes, and it's gonna wake up again. I guarantee it."

Janella frowned, studying Eugenia's pretty face and trying to understand what she was saying.

"I think you might be that one good woman, Janella. What do you think?"

Janella's jaw dropped. But she thought she understood now. It seemed Eugenia's opinion confirmed her own, the one she'd come to so long ago, when a young boy had rescued her from a hungry-looking dog.

"I think it's like *Beauty and the Beast*," she ventured, speaking slowly, watching Eugenia's face for her reactions. "He's really just a prince in disguise."

The smile that split the other woman's face was nearly blinding. She clapped her hands together, then reached out to clasp Janella's. "I just knew you and I would hit it off," she said. "It took me months to figure Thomas out, and here you've done it in a couple of days. You're a godsend, Janella."

Janella couldn't help but smile back. She was so relieved to know that this woman agreed with her about Thomas. Janella thought something had hurt him, and that he was hiding away, beneath a callous mask, just to keep from being hurt again.

"Eugenia..." She licked her lips and forced herself to go on. "You are my friend now, correct?"

"Absolutely!"

"Then I may ask you a... personal question?"

"You can ask me anything, hon. Go ahead, what is it?"

Janella stiffened her spine, met the other woman's gaze head-on. "How can I make Thomas want me?"

Eugenia lowered her head a bit, a slow smile spreading across her lips. She rubbed her hands together. "You've come to the right place, hon. The doctor isn't gonna know what hit him."

Janella came out as soon as Thomas pulled in. She didn't wait for him to shut the Jeep off or get out. She just climbed in, slung the bag she was carrying into the back and fastened her seat belt.

"What's in the bag?" He shifted into reverse, backing slowly onto the road.

"Books. You said I should read some, so Eugenia loaned me three of her favorites."

Thomas grimaced. "Don't tell me, those love stories she's always devouring."

"What's wrong with love stories?"

"I don't believe in them."

Janella's head tilted to one side, and she studied him. "Why not?"

"They aren't realistic, Janella."

"You've read many of them, then? And you are an expert?"

"Well, no—"

"Oh. Then it must be that you've been in love so many times, you know all about that."

"There's no such thing as love, Janella. Not for me, anyway. I don't need it, don't want it and won't put up with it. Does that explain it clearly enough?"

She nodded. "But Eugenia says it doesn't matter whether you want it or not. She says there is someone for everyone, one special person, and that when that person comes along, you have no choice in the matter."

"And did you check Eugenia's credentials or just buy the whole tale, hook, line and sinker?"

"What do you mean?"

"Well, she's been single all her life, Janella. Hardly an expert on affairs of the heart. She's only telling you what she wishes were true."

"Oh, no, you're wrong about that!"

"Am I?"

Janella nodded hard. "Eugenia saw a man yesterday. A stranger, who stopped outside and just glanced
in the window at her. And she said when their eyes
met, her stomach twisted and her breath caught in her
throat, and her hands began to shake." Janella looked
at him and smiled. "You should have seen her when
she talked about him, Thomas. It was wonderful to see
her eyes shine that way."

"Sounds more like food poisoning."

Thomas had to look away from her, partly because
he was driving, but mostly because of the way *her* eyes
sparkled as she talked about it. His attention no longer
riveted to those black gems, he frowned, not liking
what he'd heard.

"So who is this guy? Where's he from?"

Janella only shrugged, reaching for the bag and
pulling out a paperback. There was more in there than
books, Thomas noted, glimpsing a scrap of something sheer and black. He shifted in the seat and decided not to ask. He'd probably be better off not
knowing about Janella's underwear or whatever the
hell that was.

"Come, on, Janella, I asked a question. Who's this
guy Eugenia's all overheated about?"

"I don't know, Thomas. She says she's never seen
him before." Janella opened the paperback to the first
page and began reading.

They'd finished dinner. He was sipping fresh-
brewed coffee. Janella had set aside her paperback and
helped him clear away the dishes. She used her casted
arm as often as the uninjured one, he noticed, so he

figured she'd been right about healing in a couple of days. He'd have to take it off and check the arm later.

Now she crouched in front of the dishwasher, studying the buttons. He moved to stand behind her.

"I'll do it."

"No. I should learn to do things, Thomas. I have no servants here, and I can't expect you to care for me forever." She tipped her head back, staring into his eyes and giving him a dazzling smile. "Unless you'd like to volunteer for the job."

Thomas frowned. She looked away before he could decide if she was trying to make a joke or just talking to hear herself talk. Or maybe... Nah.

"No, thanks. I'd make a lousy servant."

She chewed her lip, studying the buttons, her fingers hovering over them. "So would I."

He lowered one hand, pushed her finger down on the right button. "That one."

"Oh." The machine whirred to life.

His hand lingered on the back of hers for a split second longer than necessary before he jerked it away and turned toward the now-spotless table. Spotless except for the stack of cookbooks Janella had piled in its center. "So tonight's going to be a crash course in cuisine?"

"I should prepare the meals from time to time," she told him. "It's only fair." She glanced at the books and sighed. "Besides, I thought I might try to see the appeal of eating animal flesh."

Her nose wrinkled at the idea. Before he thought about it, Thomas was smiling at her. He quickly remedied that and stalked into the living room. "Knock yourself out, Janella. I've got some paperwork to do anyway.''

She watched him leave, wondering again if he might want her for his own. She knew she wanted him. For some reason the idea of having sex for the first time was becoming more and more appealing to her. Especially when she read the vivid descriptions of the act in Eugenia's novel. It sounded like something very wonderful. And the notion that she'd like to try it with Thomas just wouldn't leave her alone.

Last night she'd decided the entire thing would be too complicated even to consider, but the way Eugenia had explained it, it couldn't be simpler. All Janella had to do was put on the lacy black bit of clothing Eugenia had given her, walk into Thomas's room during the night, lie down in his bed and kiss him. Janella had been worried about what to do next, but Eugenia assured her Thomas would know exactly how to handle things from there on. He only needed a "nudge" to get him started.

The question was, did Janella really want to go through with this? She began having second thoughts when she finished with the first novel. It seemed to her that the idea of sex, or *making love,* as the book called it, was more or less a declaration of undying affection. A commitment of sorts. And she still hadn't told Thomas that she wanted him as her lifelong mate. And she had no idea what he might think of the idea. She'd decided long ago that she loved him, but she was no longer so sure. In the book, it had taken a long time for that thing called love to grow between the couple. And while she was fond of Thomas and attracted to him, she wondered if what she felt would last a lifetime. She wasn't even certain she would know love if she felt it. She'd never been in love with a man, and she'd surely never witnessed that kind of tender emotion between men and women at home.

And then there was the whole other side of it. She'd have to make him love her, too. How on earth was she supposed to do that?

Janella studied a big fat cookbook for some time, trying to put thoughts of Thomas and his impending (maybe) seduction out of her mind.

The knock at the door startled her. And she glanced up to see Rosa, the receptionist, standing there. Janella felt her eyes widen. Oh, no! The woman was wearing a dress, and...and face paint. And her hair was not up in a knot as it usually was. It was loose and curly.

She opened the door and poked her head inside. "Is Thomas home?"

Thomas came into the kitchen, looked at the woman standing in the open doorway and swore under his breath.

Janella glanced from him to Rosa and back again, seeing all her plans dissolve before her eyes. If it were as easy as Eugenia had told her to seduce a man, then Rosa was surely going to succeed.

Fury rose to grip Janella, and she had a very strong urge to vent it by sending the woman flying right back through that door. But she knew that would anger Thomas, so she bit her lip and forcibly restrained herself.

She had to do something, though. What? Oh, what on earth was she going to do?

Chapter 6

Thomas blinked twice. He couldn't believe this. He'd never seen Rosa Michaels wearing anything other than jeans. Never! But here she was in a tight-fitting little halter dress that proved once and for all that the woman had a killer body. Her hair twisted and kinked in little curls down to her shoulders, and she wore more makeup than Tammy Faye.

She carried a picnic basket in one hand and a file folder in the other. She'd been wearing a hostile glare when he'd come in, one directed right at Janella. But when she saw him her smile turned sweeter than pure cane sugar.

"I found Shelly Connor's medical records on the counter before I left tonight, Thomas. I figured you'd intended to bring them home and must have forgotten, so I brought them by."

"That wasn't necessary."

Her lashes fluttered, and a hint of uncertainty crept into her eyes. "You know she's due any day now, and there's a lot here."

"Yeah, I know that." He kept his voice cold and flat. There was no way in hell he wanted to give her the slightest hint of encouragement. He did not need this bull. Not now.

"Well, I thought I could help you go over them. I brought some fried chicken and..." Her voice trailed off.

He slid a glance toward Janella. She was rising from her chair, watching the woman who'd somehow become her enemy in the space of the past two days.

"Janella and I just finished dinner."

"Oh." Her gaze fell.

"And I can manage to go over those files by myself. You're obviously dressed to go somewhere. I wouldn't want to keep you."

Rosa frowned, confused maybe. Hadn't he made himself clear enough, then? Finally, she snapped out of it and strode in as though she owned the place, setting the basket on the counter and opening the fridge.

"Well, no sense letting all this good fried chicken go to waste, is there? I'll just leave it for you." She took bowls and platters from the basket, placing them in the fridge as if she did so every day.

"Yes, Thomas," Janella put in. "You know how you love the flesh of feathered birds, especially boiled in bovine fat."

Janella's expression betrayed no hint of it, but Thomas could see the fury in those eyes. They damn near glowed with it. What the hell was her problem anyway?

Rosa met that look with a smug one of her own. "Mmm. That coffee sure smells good."

Thomas thought very seriously about turning around and leaving the room. Let the two of them kill each other if that's what they wanted. Instead, and largely for the sake of keeping a good receptionist alive and kicking, he reached for a mug and filled it. Then handed it to Rosa.

She pirouetted, smiling. "Why, thank you." She accepted the cup and sat beside him at the table. Humphrey snarled softly, and Janella reached down to pat his head and reward him with a bit of the brownie she'd been eating.

Thomas was so shocked to see it that he nearly fell off his chair.

"So, Janella, how is the house hunting going?"

Janella glanced up at Rosa, obviously irritated. "House hunting?"

"You *are* looking for a place to live, aren't you? I mean, I just assumed you wouldn't want to sponge off Thomas for longer than necessary."

"Janella is my guest, Rosa, and you're being rude as hell. You want to tell me why?"

Janella's gaze met Thomas's, softening.

Rosa looked down at her hands, then smiled at Janella. "Did that sound rude? I didn't mean it to. It's just that the whole town is talking about it. I mean, no one knows what to think, Thomas. Everyone knows what a loner you are. And I myself heard you telling Hugh Connor that you'd sooner fly to Mars than see a woman living under this roof with you."

Janella's eyes darkened, and she stared, first at Thomas, then at Rosa.

"Perhaps Thomas was referring to the women he knew then. It *was* before he'd met me. The truth is, he *insists* that I stay here with him."

"Now, just one damned minute—" Thomas began.

"Really, Janella. Don't fool yourself. Thomas would never fall for a city girl like you. I've known him a lot longer than you have, and I know that Thomas—"

"Thomas," he said, calmly setting his cup down and facing them both, "is capable of speaking for himself." He stood. "This conversation is over. Go home, Rosa."

Rosa lowered her head, obviously embarrassed. "I'd better go."

"Yes, you had better," Janella said, her voice low.

As she got to her feet, Janella eyed the filled coffee cup on the edge of the table.

Thomas saw her, gripped her shoulder, squeezed hard. "Don't even think about it."

She pouted like a kid whose candy bar had been stolen, but she restrained herself. Good thing. He hated to think what that coffee would've done to that slinky concoction Rosa wore.

He went to the door, opened it for her. "See you Monday, and we'll forget this ever happened."

Rosa shot a hate-filled glance toward Janella. "I'm sorry, Thomas, but if *she* is going to be working at the clinic, I'm going to have to give notice."

Thomas stiffened. "Giving me an ultimatum, Rosa? You claim to know me...so you ought to know better than that."

Her eyes widened a little.

"You go on home and think it over," he told her. "Then do what you have to do. But Janella stays. Here in my house, and in town at my clinic, for as long as I say."

Rosa huffed, turned and ran out of the house.

"Why do you do that?"

Thomas turned slowly, his skin still prickling with anger. Damn, nothing made him madder than people trying to tell him what to do or manipulate him into doing it.

"Do what?"

"Step into matters that do not concern you." Janella rose, came to stand right in front of him, good arm crossed with the casted one over her chest.

"Why in hell can't you try, just a little bit, to get along with the people here? Can you tell me that? Are you deliberately trying to make Rosa hate you?"

She closed her eyes, shook her head. "Men don't understand these things. I will explain for you. That *receptionist* wants you. She can't claim you because I am in her way. That is the only reason she dislikes me, Thomas."

"*Claim* me?"

Janella sighed hard, pushing one hand through her long dark hair. "Oh, I know it doesn't work that way here. She has to make you want her first. But don't you see, that's what she was trying to do. She doesn't dare to defy me or challenge me for you, so she resorts to this underhanded manner of trying to lure you to her with gifts of food and scanty clothing."

Thomas chewed his lower lip for a moment. Then he nodded thoughtfully. "So you figure Rosa thinks that you plan to…uh…*claim* me for yourself. Is that it?"

She sighed, seemingly relieved that he'd finally caught on. "Yes."

"And do you? Plan to claim me, I mean?"

She tilted her head to one side, looking him up and down. "I might. I haven't decided."

"I see." Thomas paced across the kitchen, picked up his cup from the table and carried it to the sink. As he rinsed it he spoke slowly, evenly. "Well, before you make any plans, Janella, I ought to tell you one thing."

"Yes?"

He turned slowly, slung the cup into the sink and faced her. "No one is going to claim me. Not you. Not Rosa. Nobody. Understand?"

She frowned. "Oh, Thomas, don't be foolish. I didn't say I wanted you forever. Only for sex."

He closed his eyes, gave his head a shake. "You wanna repeat that?"

"Sex," she said again. "I wish to experience it. There's no reason not to. It isn't forbidden here. And you told me yourself it's a matter of personal choice. So, my personal choice is to try it. And I would like to try it with you."

He didn't know whether to roll on the floor laughing or scream bloody murder. "No, Janella."

Her brows drew closer. "But why?"

She took a step closer to him. He took one backward.

"You told me you'd done it before. That you did it only for physical pleasure. That it didn't matter that you cared so little for the women. So why?"

Good question. Damned good question. Hell, if she was so willing to have meaningless, casual sex with him, why wasn't he jumping at the chance? He'd wanted her from the second he'd laid eyes on her. So what was the problem?

Janella answered his question before he could. Her head lowering, she whispered, "You do not desire me."

"Look, it wouldn't be smart, okay? I know how you women are. Sleep with a man once and start thinking he's yours for life. It isn't gonna happen, Janella. If I want sex, I'll get it from a stranger, and if you want some man to *claim*, you'd better look elsewhere."

She blinked in shock, took an unsteady step backward. Then her face changed. Pure undiluted rage twisted her features, and her eyes just about spat fire. "I could have you in chains for that."

"Not here, you couldn't. Hell, it's no wonder you left your planet. What a warped frigging place it must have been."

She clenched her fists, nails digging into her palms, knuckles whitening. Damn, she was mad enough to kill. Her body trembled as she fought a visible battle for control. The dishes on the table rattled, the table itself vibrating beneath them. She grated her teeth, squeezed her eyes tight. One of the cupboard doors swung open, the dishes inside jostling near the edge of the shelf. The lights flickered.

Finally, she drew a deep breath, held it a long time and released it all at once. Then she turned, slammed out of the house, and the dishes settled down again.

Thomas swore as he watched her stride away from the house, across the lawn, toward the stubbly wheat field. Damn, she had a temper. He shook his head, feeling an odd, disconnected sense of unreality float through his mind. Just what the extent of her powers might be, he had no clue. But he suddenly had a feeling she wouldn't be a good person to cross. If he were anyone other than who he was, he might have thought twice about arousing that anger again. But being Thomas, he didn't.

She should have yelled, vented a little. He thought that as he shoved the dishes back into the cupboard and closed the door. Even though she was dead wrong and needed a good lesson in humility, she should have vented a little.

She sure as all hell didn't take rejection very well. He supposed she was used to getting everything she wanted back up there on Krypton, where she was some kind of princess or something.

He went to the door, thought about going after her, then decided against it. Let her have some time to cool off. He turned back to the kitchen. Maybe he'd try to explain things to her a little more gently when she came back.

If she came back.

He managed to hang tough for two hours. Even when the sun went down and darkness settled in like a shroud. But when the thunder rumbled in the distance and the rain started, he lost his indifference again.

Janella sat at the edge of the charred ground in the woods, and she let the tears of frustration and rage flow freely. Never had she been so utterly alone. And so out of place! No one here understood her. And it seemed they never would. At home, things had been so simple. The men there respected her. She was the daughter of their ruler, the next queen of the planet, after all. They didn't mind their lot in life. It was the natural order of things, the way she saw it. The men were physically stronger and more adept at labor. The women were the ruling class. But they treated their men well, gave them all they needed and even grew fond of them sometimes. Why, Janella's mother had even asked her father's opinion on the running of the world a time or two.

At home, the males had been eager to gain Janella's attention, all of them hoping to be the one she chose as her own. But here, here she was treated no better than that dog Humphrey. And Thomas...he didn't even want her! Eugenia had been wrong about that. And Janella would be hung by her hair before she'd humble herself to ask him again. She could only thank the fates that she had told him she didn't want him forever. It would have hurt ten times as much if she'd offered her heart, told him she was all but certain that she loved him, and he'd rejected what she offered. She'd lied, of course. She did want him forever. Oh, it was all so confusing. No wonder the people in the movies took such a long time before declaring their feelings.

She missed home. She missed her father, had missed him most of her life. He would have understood these feelings. He and no one else. Because he had emotions, too, and refused to erase them from his heart. Janella felt more alone than she ever had, and yet, she was glad to be able to release her roiling emotions here, where no one would condemn her for her weakness. Even when the rains came to cool her heated skin, she didn't move from the spot. She'd die before she'd return to that horrible renegade male and his radical notions.

She lowered her head into the pillow of her arms and let her emotions run free. Better to cleanse herself of them now, and be more in control later.

One thing was certain. Thomas didn't want her. Not in the least. He'd probably only taken care of her, let her stay with him, from some sense of duty. He must not care for her any more than he did for his patients.

And here she'd been thinking he truly did care for them, that his coldness was only a disguise.

But she'd obviously been mistaken about that. He didn't care. Not for anyone, but most especially not for her. And she wouldn't spend one more night in a place where she was so clearly unwanted.

"Thomas Duffy?"

Thomas gave a sharp nod, eyeing the stranger who stood on his front porch. He was tall, lean. He wore his brown hair long for a man of his age, but it suited the close-cropped, gray speckled beard on his chin. And his warm brown eyes were friendly, despite Thomas's obvious impatience. He'd been on his way to find Janella and bring her in out of the rain. Instead, he'd been waylaid by this stranger.

"I need a word with you, Dr. Duffy. Do you have a moment?"

"No. I was just on my way out."

"I can see that. Believe me this is important. I promise, I'll be brief."

Thomas glanced past him to the cloud-veiled night sky, the pouring rain. He saw lightning flash in the distance. "I really have to go, mister—"

"It's about Janella."

Thomas's attention was caught. "Maybe you'd better tell me who the hell you are."

The man nodded, smiling gently. "My name is Alex Vrooman. And before you get hostile, you should know that I'm on your side in this. But there are some others in Sumac who aren't."

"Look, I really don't know what you're talking about, so—"

"Yes, you do. Dr. Duffy, it's admirable of you to try to protect her, but I'm not the enemy here."

Thomas shook his head and moved to walk past the stranger.

"I know about the ship, Thomas. And the crash. I know you found Janella in the woods beyond this farm. I know where she comes from. I know all of it."

Thomas blinked in shock, refusing to turn and face the man, knowing his expression would betray him.

"They know, too. Or at least, they suspect."

He did turn now. "Who?"

"A man by the name of Halloway. He's with military intelligence. If he gets his hands on Janella, Dr. Duffy, I'm afraid..." He lowered his eyes, shook his head. "It wouldn't be good."

Thomas grabbed the man's arm. "What do you mean, it wouldn't be good."

Alex Vrooman sighed. "Despite our efforts to prevent it, Dr. Duffy, the last extraterrestrial captured by our wonderful government died in captivity. Probably as a result of the constant experiments performed on him. We tried to get to him before Halloway, but—"

"Who the hell are 'we,' Vrooman?"

"ETPN," he said softly. "Extraterrestrial Protective Network."

"For crying out loud." Thomas rolled his eyes, pushed a hand through his hair and turned in a slow circle. "You expect me to *believe* this crap?"

"There's no time to convince you right now, Duffy. I have to know whether there's any evidence of that crash in those woods?"

"There was no crash in those woods, Mr. Vrooman."

"I realize the craft probably appeared to vanish. But there might be ashes, or charred ground, and if Halloway finds—"

"Look, I don't know any Halloway, and if I did, I sure wouldn't let him go traipsing through my woodlot looking for flying saucers, okay? Feel better now?"

Vrooman placed a firm hand on Thomas's shoulder. "He's traipsing through your woodlot right now, Dr. Duffy. Is there anything for him to find?"

The blood rushed to Thomas's feet. He blinked in shock at the man, saw the intensity in those eyes, and swore fluently. "Janella's out there."

"My God."

She had no idea how long she'd been sitting in the rain, when a hand on her shoulder brought her head up fast. Thomas stood, dripping wet, staring down at her.

"You okay?"

She was glad of the rain, to hide the dampness of tears on her face. She only nodded and looked back toward the burned ground.

"Come back to the house, Janella. It isn't good to sit in the rain. It's cold tonight."

"You made it clear you don't want me there, Thomas. I'll trouble you no longer." She spoke without looking at him, still afraid he'd see signs of her emotional reaction to his rejection. It was only her pride that was wounded. Nothing more.

"I didn't say I didn't want you there."

"Didn't you?"

His hand closed on her arm, and he pulled her to her feet roughly. "You know damn well I didn't. Now, come on, I'm not going to stand here in the pouring rain arguing with you."

She caught her breath as he tugged at her, and jerked her arm free. "You dare—"

"You're damned right I dare." He pulled again, forcing her to walk along at his side.

And again she jerked her arm free of his grasp.

He stared at her, his eyes boring holes through hers, it seemed. And she felt a ripple of fear at the anger she saw there. "Fine. Have it your way." Before she could guess his intent, he'd grabbed her in his unyielding arms. He scooped her up off her feet, flipped her right over his shoulder and, despite her howl of protest or the blows she rained on his back and shoulders, began trudging back through the woods.

Her struggles amounted to nothing. Like battling the wind. So she gave them up. And when she quieted, he lowered her to the ground, but held her upper arms in his hands. "You ready to move under your own steam now, princess?"

"I despise you."

"Yeah, well, it's mutual. So are you walking or riding?"

She glared at him, swiped the wet hair out of her eyes and turned to trudge off toward the house. She would claw his eyes out at the very first opportunity. Why she'd ever thought him a decent man, she couldn't begin to imagine.

He quickly caught up to her, walking along at her side. They'd moved on in utter silence, but for no more than a few steps. She stopped when she heard voices floating through the rain toward them. Glancing at Thomas, she saw that he'd heard them, too. He frowned hard, staring into the distance, and following his gaze, Janella saw the beams of light moving through the trees.

From somewhere a voice called. "Anything?"

"Not a damned thing. Are you sure about the location?"

"This is it. Has to be. The witnesses claim this is where they saw it go down."

The lights moved farther, and Janella stiffened as she watched them pass. Without realizing it, she'd gripped Thomas's arm.

He looked down at her, his face grim. The men were heading toward the charred ground, and if they found it, there would be questions. Janella felt trapped. Who were they? What would happen if they discovered . . .

"Hold up there!" Thomas's loud, deep voice boomed through the rainy night. The lights stopped moving, turned in their direction. "Stay here," he whispered. With one glance at her, Thomas started forward.

Janella followed.

The men came this way, and only stopped when face-to-face with Thomas. There were three, covered head to toe in dark-blue raincoats. One smiled and nodded at Thomas. "What can I do for you, mister?"

"I ought to be the one asking that, seeing as it's my property you boys are tromping all over. Who the hell are you and what are you doing out here?"

The men glanced at one another. But it was the same one, the leader, it seemed, who replied. "Look, buddy, we don't want any trouble. We're with the air force. We had a ... a satellite crash somewhere in this area, and we have to find it."

Thomas nodded. "Not tonight, you don't. Hit the road, pal."

"I'm afraid—"

"Unless you have some kind of search warrant," Thomas cut in, "get the hell off my land. Now."

"We can get one, Duffy. That is who you are, isn't it? I want to get the name right when I file charges."

Thomas didn't even flinch. "Two f's, one y. Be sure and spell it right."

The man glared at Thomas for a long moment. But then his gaze shifted, and when it fell on Janella she felt real fear ripple over her spine. He smiled at her, put out a hand. "Special Investigator Jack Halloway, ma'am. And you are ... ?"

Thomas swung his head around and swore softly. She saw the anger in his eyes. So she was even more perplexed when he reached for her, caught her hand

and drew her close to his side. His hand around hers was warm and strong, and she found herself clinging to it, ignoring the one the other man held out to her. The one she felt certain could destroy her.

"None of your business, Halloway," Thomas said. And his hand fell away from hers, only to encircle her waist and pull her tight to his side.

"Got something to hide, do you, Duffy? Word around town is, this lady showed up out of nowhere. Same night that... test flight went down, wasn't it, boys?"

"Y-you said it was a satellite," Janella whispered. Her voice had deserted her.

"Did I? Well, who knows? *Something* crashed here two nights ago. I'll know for sure what it was when I find the site. And I will find it. Say, were you here when it happened? Did you see anything?"

He knew. It was in his smile. Something wild and frightened broke loose inside her and Janella suddenly wanted to send a tree toppling down to crush this frightening man. Fear made her energy jump and leap inside her mind, and she heard the leaves rustling, the branches overhead twitching in motion, though there was no breeze. She caught herself, forced herself calm. The trees stilled, and she prayed the men hadn't noticed her slip.

"Come on, now, miss. You can tell me. Who are you *really?*"

"I—"

"She's my wife."

Janella blinked in shock at the declaration that seemed to leap from Thomas's lips without his consent.

"I suppose you can prove that?"

Thomas's fingers opened on her waist, exerting gentle pressure. A warning. She was shivering. She hadn't realized it until his warmth seeped into her skin and gradually eased the chill.

"I don't think I have to," Thomas went on, his voice deadly but calm.

"I'm afraid you do."

Thomas's chin lifted. His eyes shot fury. "You want proof, you try finding it. And good luck. We were married on Karicau by the village priest, but no one was really in power at the time, and he was taken out by a sniper. The church has been burned out so many times there's probably not a record left anywhere. It's a mess over there, you know."

"So I've heard."

"I returned six months ago, and Janella was only able to join me recently."

"And I'll just bet she came without a visa. Probably has no birth certificate, either. And it's all a coincidence, right?"

"She's my wife. That makes her a citizen."

Halloway eyed her, doubting, she knew. She called on her years of schooling at home and blurted a string of questions in a perfect Karicau dialect. Halloway blinked in apparent shock, and just a little of the doubt left his eyes. Not all of it, though.

Thomas frowned down at her, but the surprise on his face was quickly concealed. "In English, honey. How many times have I told you?"

"Come on, Duffy. You've got no proof of any of this. And *that* makes her an illegal alien. Maybe I ought to call my buddy at Immigration."

"She'll be legal soon enough."

Halloway smirked. "Planning a wedding, are you?"

Thomas shrugged, hugging her closer. "Hell, it'll be easier than tracking down proof of the first one. Now, if your curiosity is satisfied, would you mind getting the hell out of here before I'm forced to turn my dog loose?"

Halloway fixed his penetrating gaze on Janella, staring so hard she shuddered.

Thomas felt it; she knew he did. "Well? Can I walk you boys to your car?"

"How is it no one in this fly speck of a town knows about their local doctor's new wife?"

"Because that's the way I wanted it. My private life is private, Halloway. I didn't feel the need to post an announcement on the town bulletin board."

"I know you're lying."

"So prove it."

"Oh, don't worry. I will. You have a nice night, Duffy. I'll have a search warrant here in twenty-four hours."

"Well, you just come on back when you do. I might even help you look for your missing . . . whatever it was."

The man muttered, but turned to those behind him and inclined his head. All three walked behind Thomas and Janella out of the woods. They veered across the wheat field, toward the road where their car was parked, and Thomas stood, waiting until they'd gotten in and driven away, before turning to her once more.

"They know, Thomas. They know about the ship and the crash and . . . and about *me*."

"They suspect. They don't *know* anything, and they damned well aren't going to."

She stared up into his eyes, confused, and more frightened than she could remember ever having been in her life. "But you told them—"

"Forget what I told them, Janella." He kept his arm around her shoulders as they headed back toward the house. "We've got more important things to worry about, like what we're going to do when they show up tomorrow night with that search warrant."

There was a stranger waiting in the kitchen when they returned. Janella had never seen him before, and she was afraid at first. But Thomas glanced down at her, reassurance in his eyes.

"It's okay, Janella." He looked at the man, who sat at the kitchen table sipping tea, and added, "At least, I'm relatively sure it is."

The man rose slowly. He was very tall, and quite thin. And his brown eyes took her in with something like awe. He smiled at her, lifted a hand. "You wouldn't believe how pleased I am to meet you, Janella."

He came forward slowly. She cringed a little closer to Thomas. Humphrey lunged from under the table to take up a stance at her opposite side. He growled a soft warning to the man, as Janella took the hand the man offered.

"Welcome," the stranger said.

She blinked, frowning at the unlined face, the neat beard and once again at those brown eyes. "Who are you?"

"Alex Vrooman. I'm here to help you."

Janella looked at Thomas, who only shook his head. "We have all night to talk to Mr. Vrooman—"

"'Alex,' please."

"You're soaking wet, Janella. Why don't you go on upstairs, get into some dry clothes?"

She blinked away some of the fear. "You're as wet as I am, Thomas."

He pushed the hair away from her face. "Go on. I'll be up in a minute."

She nodded and turned to leave them.

Chapter 7

Thomas watched her go, his gut churning. The frigging iron wall he'd been struggling to keep between them had damn near crumbled to dust. It was the fear in her eyes. Fear he knew was justified. Hell, he could be as cold as he wanted when she was arrogant and demanding. Not when she looked like a doe caught in headlights, though. He might as well get used to it, he supposed. He was all she had right now. She needed him, and there was no way around that. His practical mind had deserted him out there in the woods tonight, and his damned emotional side—that impulsive kid inside who thought of himself as her knight in shining armor—had dug him into a pit. He'd have a hell of a time getting out of it.

Facing Vrooman, he squared his shoulders, ready to do battle for the damn damsel upstairs.

"You might as well know up front, Vrooman, if I find out you're lying, if you do anything to hurt her—"

"I only want to help her." Vrooman stepped up to Thomas, clasped his shoulder in a strong grip. "I'm on your side in this, Thomas. Would I have warned you about Halloway and his men if I wasn't?"

"I'm not sure." Thomas took careful stock of the man's face, the kind eyes. He wanted to believe Vrooman was sincere, but he wasn't about to take any chances with Janella's safety. He nodded toward the table, and Vrooman sat, picking up his forgotten tea. "Just what do you think you can do to help us?" Thomas asked, taking the seat across from him.

"I can keep you informed about Halloway and his men. What they're up to, what they suspect, what they plan."

Thomas felt his eyes narrow. "How?"

"ETPN is a large organization, Thomas. We have people keeping tabs on the government. I'm afraid I can't divulge more than that without risking some of my colleagues. Just believe me when I say, we know what we're doing. We've had to do it before."

"*What?*"

Vrooman smiled, carefully setting his cup on the table. "Janella isn't the first. There are others, more than you'd believe. When things settle down and Halloway's attention is diverted, I'll put her in contact with them."

Thomas only stared, feeling as if he'd been struck between the eyes with a two-by-four. "Others?"

"Mmm, many others." Vrooman sipped, licked his lips, replaced the cup. "They all have one thing in common. They're high-strung, highly emotional. It was pure hell for them at home.''

"Why's that?"

Thomas turned at the sound of footsteps. Janella stood in the doorway, hair damp and clinging to her neck and shoulders. She wore his blue terry robe, and her eyes were misty.

"There are others?" Her voice was a squeaky whisper.

Vrooman nodded, and Thomas saw her grip the door frame for support.

"Where?" She blinked, but tears shimmered in her eyes all the same.

Dammit. If Vrooman was lying to her Thomas would kill the bastard.

"I can't tell you just yet, Janella. For their protection. Not until Halloway decides you're just another earthling, like Thomas and me." He grinned at her, and she smiled back, nodding hard.

Thomas shook his head. Man, this was getting harder to swallow by the second. "Someone want to explain this to me?" He turned to Janella. "What's so terrible about your planet that it drives people to leave everything and fly off to parts unknown?"

Janella lowered her head. Thomas looked to Vrooman for the answers, but found none.

"It's up to Janella to tell you about that, Thomas. When she's ready. For now, I think I ought to go. You both need some time to digest all of this. We'll talk again tomorrow."

Thomas dragged his gaze away from Janella's face. She looked almost guilty, but he couldn't imagine why. "Vrooman, wait. Halloway will be back tomorrow with a search warrant. What the hell am I supposed to do about that?''

Vrooman nodded thoughtfully, rubbing his chin with one hand. "Wouldn't do to let them find evidence to support their theory. Tell me, does anything remain of the ship?''

"No.''

"Good." He nodded, rising from his chair, pacing slowly. "Then you only need to worry about the ground. The topsoil is charred black, isn't it?''

Thomas nodded, certain now that Vrooman hadn't been lying when he'd said he'd dealt with situations like this before. How else could he know about that blackened earth?

"The topsoil ought to be removed, or at least plowed under, as deeply as possible," Vrooman said. "They won't see any sign of the landing, and with luck, their soil samples will show nothing unusual.''

"I hope the hell you're right about that." Thomas turned to Janella as she came the rest of the way into the room, walked right up to Vrooman and stared into his eyes. Her own were so intense it seemed she was searching his soul.

"What will they do to me if they find out?" The fear in her voice was palpable, and it made Thomas want to bundle her into the Jeep and take her as far away from Halloway and Vrooman and all of this bull as he could get her.

Vrooman glanced away from her, toward Thomas. Thomas gave his head a slight shake. *Tell her what you told me and I'll break your jaw.*

Vrooman's slight nod said he'd read the message, loud and clear. He rose, patting Janella's shoulder.

"We aren't going to have to find out, Janella. Don't worry." He moved toward the door, pausing with one hand on the knob. "She needs to be vaccinated against polio, Thomas. Be sure it's an inactive vaccine, and give her a child's dose. It won't hurt her. They seem to be immune to most of our diseases, but that one can be fatal. Also, red meat seems to disagree with them. And watch out for MSGs."

Thomas nodded. "What about medications?"

"Hard to say," Vrooman said. "We only found out about the other things by accident. We don't treat them like guinea pigs, you know." He tilted his head, looking at Janella for a long moment. "It's better to avoid anything you're unsure of. Think holistic, Thomas. Don't take any chances with her health."

"I don't intend to."

With a sharp nod, Vrooman left, and Thomas turned to find Janella sagging, hands clasping the back of a chair. He caught her shoulders, turned her around, studied her face, and searched within himself for his iron wall.

The damn thing was nowhere in sight.

"You all right?"

She nodded, but he doubted her answer. She looked exhausted, scared, confused and a hundred other things he couldn't put a name to.

"Come on, kid. Upstairs with you. I think a nice hot bath and then straight to bed."

She lifted her head, stared into his eyes. "You told those men I was your wife."

"I told *you* to forget about what I told those men."

"But it isn't true."

"No, it isn't. Hell, Janella, I had to come up with something fast. It was the first thing that popped into my head."

She blinked twice, and he thought if he didn't look away those wide black eyes of hers were going to suck the soul right out of his body and chain it up somewhere inside hers.

He tried, but couldn't.

"What will happen when they find out that you lied to them?"

"They aren't going to find out."

"But—"

"Janella, will you just trust me? I'll take care of this."

She shook her head. "I don't see how you can. You told them we were to be married. When we aren't, they'll know—"

"They aren't going to stick around that long. Hell, Janella, maybe Alex Vrooman will whisk you off to wherever the rest of your people are living. Maybe Halloway will lose interest. You're worrying about things that haven't happened yet."

Her eyes grew even wider, though he hadn't believed it possible. Her lips trembled. "You...you think I should go to them? To the others?" Her voice came out tight, as if her throat had constricted and was squeezing the words.

"I figured you'd want to go to them. You do, don't you?"

Her chin fell to her chest, hair veiling her face as she turned away from him. "With all that's happened, Thomas, our earlier conversation slipped my mind. Foolish of me to forget, wasn't it?"

She started for the stairs. Thomas caught her by her good arm, stopping her. "To forget what, Janella? What are you talking about?"

Without facing him, she shook her head. "Don't concern yourself about me any longer, Thomas. I'll be out of your house, out of your life, just as soon as Alex Vrooman tells me where to go." She tugged her arm free of his grip and tiredly mounted the stairs.

Thomas didn't follow her.

He didn't want her! How had she forgotten that, even for a moment?

Janella fell face first onto the bed, clutching the pillows in her fists. When he'd told those men he would marry her, when he'd pulled her close to his side and held her and called her "honey" with so much affection in his voice, she'd actually believed it.

More than believed it. She'd *reveled* in it.

She'd been a fool. A blind, frightened little girl clinging to the false security, the make-believe love of a man who cared less for her than for his dog. Why did it hurt her so much? Why, when she'd known him for such a short time, did it pain her to know he felt nothing for her? He wanted no woman in his life, didn't believe in love at all. He was like the people she'd run away from, emotionless, cold, unfeeling. Why would she even want the affection of a man like him?

But she did. She did want it, and it surprised her to realize just how much. It hadn't been simple anger she'd felt toward Rosa, but jealousy. All her life she'd thought of Thomas as the man who would be her own.

WE'VE GOT 5 FREE GIFTS FOR YOU!
FIND OUT <u>INSTANTLY</u> WHAT YOU
GET WITH THE

CARNIVAL WHEEL

▼ SCRATCH-OFF GAME! ▼

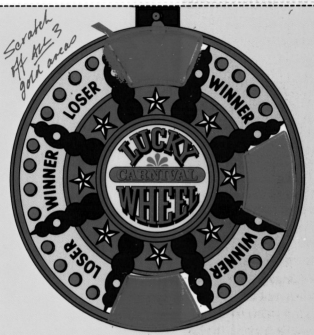

Scratch off ALL 3 gold areas

YES! I have scratched off the 3 Gold Areas above. Please send me all the gifts for which I qualify. I understand I am under no obligation to purchase any books, as explained on the back and on the opposite page.

245 CIS ASU6
(U-SIL-IM-04/95)

NAME

ADDRESS   APT.

CITY   STATE   ZIP

Offer limited to one per household and not valid to current Silhouette Intimate Moments® subscribers. All orders subject to approval.
©1991 Harlequin Enterprises Limited   **Printed in U.S.A.**

DETACH AND MAIL CARD TODAY!

THE SILHOUETTE READER SERVICE™: HERE'S HOW IT WORKS

Accepting free books places you under no obligation to buy anything. You may keep the books and gift and return the shipping statement marked "cancel". If you do not cancel, about a month later we will send you 6 additional novels, and bill you just $2.89 each plus 25¢ delivery and applicable sales tax, if any.* That's the complete price, and—compared to cover prices of $3.75 each—quite a bargain! You may cancel at any time, but if you choose to continue, every month we'll send you 6 more books, which you may either purchase at the discount price…or return at our expense and cancel your subscription.

*Terms and prices subject to change without notice. Sales tax applicable in N.Y.

If offer card is missing, write to: Silhouette Reader Service, 3010 Walden Ave., P.O. Box 1867, Buffalo, NY 14269-1867

BUSINESS REPLY MAIL

FIRST CLASS MAIL   PERMIT NO. 717   BUFFALO, NY

POSTAGE WILL BE PAID BY ADDRESSEE

SILHOUETTE READER SERVICE
3010 WALDEN AVE
PO BOX 1867
BUFFALO NY 14240-9952

NO POSTAGE
NECESSARY
IF MAILED
IN THE
UNITED STATES

Ever since that night when he'd rescued her in the woods, so long ago.

She sat up, sniffling and reaching into the drawer for the small wooden trinket he'd given her then. Lovingly, she stroked the smooth grain of the wood, her fingers caressing Thomas's initials. He'd become her ideal that night, and she'd stupidly spent years longing for his love, his touch. It had never occurred to her that he wouldn't return her feelings. The reality of that had only hit her with his cruel rejection. And it hurt more than she believed possible.

She told herself her feelings for Thomas were false. That he'd been the only person she'd known since coming here. That his rescuing of her so long ago had made him a romantic hero in her mind, and that she clung to him now from a need of security more than from any real caring.

She didn't believe what she was telling herself, however. And it didn't ease the ache in her heart a bit. She'd spent her whole life waiting for the day when she could come to him. Now she had to leave him. It was what he wanted. He'd made that plain enough. And she knew he wouldn't change his mind.

Thomas didn't sleep. He couldn't. His pacing and frustration finally led him to his room, which had somehow become Janella's. He'd been sleeping in Dad's old bedroom since he'd found her.

She lay still, eyes red and swollen, tear tracks still traceable on her cheeks.

Had he caused her tears? Hell, he didn't know. She might have cried out of fear of discovery, or maybe from the sheer joy of knowing she wasn't as alone here as she'd thought.

That's right, she wasn't alone. He reminded himself of that. Before, he'd been all she had. She'd needed him. Now she knew there were others like her here. And there was Alex Vrooman and his organization. She could probably get along just fine without some country doctor's pitiful help.

Hadn't she told him she wanted to leave?

No. She'd said she would leave because he wanted it. And she was right. He did want it. The sooner she was out of his life, the sooner he could repair the damage to his emotion-proof wall and get things back to normal. He didn't like having her here, didn't like the feeling that he was starting to care about her far more than was wise. Hell, she was living proof of what that kind of caring led to. She was walking away, wasn't she?

And he was going to miss her like hell, wasn't he?

He forced his gaze away from her, but it did nothing to ease the ridiculous sting behind his eyes. And looking at the floor only brought to attention the little bag she'd brought home from The Pink Petunia. It lay on its side, books and a black satin strap spilling out. In spite of himself, Thomas reached down, hooked a finger through that strap and pulled the garment out.

The teddy was damn near transparent, with high-cut leg openings and a low-cut neckline.

Thomas dropped it, spun for the door and left the room as fast as was humanly possible. In the hall, he pulled the door shut, leaned back against it, eyes closed, teeth grating.

"Damn, damn, damn."

Drawing an uneven breath, he steeled himself against the images that kept floating through his mind. Images of Janella in that black teddy. Of her hands on his skin, his lips on her mouth.

His first instincts had been correct. The sooner she got the hell out of his life, the better.

The telephone's shrill ring didn't wake him, because he hadn't been asleep. He'd been lying on his back, staring at the ceiling and contemplating what would be so terrible about letting Janella stay right where she was. Stupid thought. She probably didn't even *want* to stay, but the idea kept coming back to him, no matter how he tried to banish it.

He snatched up the cordless, having taken it to bed with him out of habit.

"Thomas? It's Eugenia, hon. You'd better get over here, and I do mean now."

His senses stood alert and he sat up in bed. "What is it, 'Genia. You okay?"

"Well now, Thomas 'Hard-nose' Duffy, is that concern I hear in your voice? You softy, you. I'm fine." Thomas grimaced into the mouthpiece, but she rushed on. "It's Shelly Connor. She was on her way back from visiting Hugh at the hospital, and she went into labor."

"Oh, hell. Well, pop her into your car and I'll meet you back at Saint Luke's."

"I don't think so, Thomas. She's—" A piercing shriek coming from somewhere beyond her interrupted her words.

"Holy crap," Thomas muttered.

"I have to go, Thomas. Get your butt over here, *pronto.*"

The receiver clicked in his ear. Thomas hung up, dove into his clothes and ran into the hall. Janella was there, eyes still red, but dry now. He assumed the phone most have jarred her awake. He wished it hadn't. Looking at her fresh from bed, in his rumpled bathrobe, with mussed hair and half-lidded eyes, was only distracting him from the matter at hand.

"Something is wrong," she said softly.

"Shelly's having her baby. Any minute now by the sounds of it. I have to go."

"I want to come with you." She turned and dashed into the bedroom before he could argue. Thomas followed, about to tell her there was no time to wait. Then he wished he hadn't. She shed the robe and stood stark naked in front of an open dresser drawer, pawing through it, yanking out a pair of jeans. He stood behind her, staring like an idiot at her bare legs and the perfect curve of her backside, her slender waist. And when he looked away from that it was only to see the front of her reflected in the mirror. Her eyes met his in the glass, held them for a moment, then tore free.

She bent and stepped into the jeans, yanked them up over her hips. She dipped back into the drawer for a T-shirt, pulled it over her head. Grabbing her shoes from the floor, she came to him.

He didn't move out of the doorway. She stood there, looking up at him, so tousled and beautiful that for a second he could think of nothing but pulling her into his arms and kissing the living hell out of her.

Damn. What was wrong with him?

"Come on. We'd better hurry." And why was his voice so damned hoarse? He turned away, but not before he was sure she'd seen the desire in his eyes. And he was damned if he hadn't seen the same thing shining right back at him from hers.

She was pretty and young. Small and blond. But her hair clung in straggles to her sweat-dampened face, and her beautiful features contorted in pain.

Janella rushed to the bedside without forethought. She'd never witnessed childbirth, but at home it was done surgically, while the mother lay unconscious and unaware. She was spared the pain of natural birth and the other pain that came later, as those in attendance—representatives of the ruling house—decided whether the child was sound enough to accept, or flawed, in which case its life would end more quickly than it had begun. Those were the only two skills needed by men of medicine on her planet.

Eugenia left her spot at Shelly's side to assist Thomas near the foot of the bed. But Janella was only dimly aware of their presence there. She knew little other than the pain of the woman on the bed, and she focused on nothing other than easing it.

Janella bent over her, placed her hands on either side of Shelly's head, palms absorbing the sticky sweat.

Shelly screamed.

"Dammit," Thomas muttered. "She's not big enough. We ought to do a C-section, but there isn't time to get her to the hospital."

"The baby's crowning, Thomas. I don't think Shelly can stand—"

Shelly shrieked in agony, arching off the bed.

Janella leaned in close to her face. "Open your eyes, Shelly. Open them. Look at me. Right into my eyes."

Shelly's eyes fluttered open, and Janella held her pain-clouded gaze. She searched those eyes, massaging Shelly's temples and chanting in her own tongue, her voice a bare whisper as she sought to draw the pain out of Shelly's body, to ease the woman's suffering.

Another contraction came, and Janella felt its echo in her own abdomen as her mind sought to meld with Shelly's. Her muscles clenched and she caught her breath, but didn't close her eyes. Shelly blinked, panting, her eyes clearing just a little. She started to look away, but Janella held her face.

"Keep looking at me, Shelly. I can help you through this. Don't look away."

Shelly did, and as another contraction hit her, she gasped, but didn't scream. Janella felt it more strongly this time and again caught her breath, but forced her gaze to remain fixed on Shelly's. Her hands on Shelly's face trembled.

"It's coming," Thomas shouted. "You have to push now, Shelly. Come on, I know it hurts, but—"

Shelly grated her teeth and pushed. Janella felt as if she were being ripped apart from within. She bit her lip to keep from making a sound and probed still deeper into the young woman's mind, sharing her pain, easing it.

Shelly sat up in the bed, her back braced on the headboard, knees bent, feet digging into the mattress. She never looked away from Janella. Janella sat on the bed's edge, hands to Shelly's temples, eyes locked in place. Shelly pushed again, and Janella grated her teeth, sending all of her energies into the young mother, trying to give her strength and endurance. On and on the pains came, until they blended into one unending force. Shelly clung to Janella's shoulders as powerfully as to her gaze, her own tear filled and grateful and confused. She grated her teeth as she pushed, her fingers sinking into Janella's skin. Their faces only inches apart, both women panted in cosmic synchronization, eyes intense, sharing the pain.

And then it eased all of the sudden.

Shelly fell back onto the pillows. Janella slid from the bed, where she'd been sitting, to kneel on the floor, head bowed. She heard the baby's first wheezy cry, and then silence. Her head came up slowly, eyes focused on the unmoving newborn in Thomas's arms.

"Dammit," he muttered, snipping the cord and rubbing the child vigorously. "Come on, dammit!"

Janella pulled herself to her feet; leaning on the bed for support, she moved to the foot of it.

The child's skin was a soft blue beneath the ghostly white film. Shelly sat up again, moaning "No," her gaze pinned to the baby.

Thomas cradled the child with one arm, sweeping a finger into its mouth. Janella drew closer. Please, she begged in silence, please.

"She's not breathing!" Shelly cried. "Thomas, she's not—"

Thomas bent over the still child, covering the baby's mouth and nose with his lips, blowing gentle puffs into the tiny lungs. When he lifted his head, he used two fingers to pump the child's chest, then bent to blow again.

"Come on, sweetheart," he whispered. "Come on, dammit, come on." His eyes were intense as he kept ministering to the infant. He kept working as Shelly's sobs grew louder and she crawled toward the foot of the bed.

"Thomas, please! Please don't let her—"

The baby gurgled. A hoarse sound, like a wheezy gasp, instigated utter silence in the room. Every eye pinned to that child. And then it began to cry like a lamb for its mother.

Shelly doubled over on the bed, sobbing so hard her entire body shook with it. Janella sank onto the mattress, tears filling her eyes. And through the blur of them, she saw Thomas's eyes filling, as well, and a crooked smile tugging at his lips.

Eugenia was bubbling with joy when the siren screamed louder, then warbled to a stop out front. The door burst open and paramedics rushed inside. A medic took the baby from Shelly's arms. Then others transferred Shelly to a gurney and wheeled her out of the room. But as it passed, she reached out to clasp Thomas's hand. She didn't speak, but her eyes gleamed her gratitude.

He gave her hand a squeeze. "See you at the hospital, Shel." Then she was carried past him and out of the house.

Thomas turned to study Janella, still unsure what he'd just witnessed. Somehow, in some weird, damn near scary way, Janella had eased Shelly's pain. He knew it without being told. And he could see the effort it had cost her. Exhaustion was written all over her face.

"Are you all right?"

She nodded, watching the medics as they bundled Shelly and the baby into the back of the ambulance outside.

"Fine, Thomas. But the baby?"

She looked truly worried. "The baby will be okay. Her lungs are a little underdeveloped, and she's small. She'll need intensive care for a while, but I think she'll be fine in a couple of weeks." He put a hand on her face, pushed her hair away, caught the tear that fell.

She shook her head slowly, staring at him with something like wonder in her eyes.

"Janella, I'm not sure what just happened here, but—"

"What happened here was a miracle, Thomas." Her smile was watery as more tears spilled over. "The baby... You gave her life. You brought her back. You—"

He closed his eyes to block out the adoration in hers. "I did what I'm trained to do. That's all."

"You cried when she breathed again. I saw you."

"You're hallucinating. And I wasn't talking about what I did. I was talking about what you did. You... How the hell did you—"

The siren's scream made him stop. "We'll talk about it later. I have to go to the hospital now, Janella. Stay here." Again he ran his hand over her face. "Rest. You look like hell. Are you sure you're okay?"

Instead of answering him, she leaned up and pressed her mouth to his. Her eyes fell closed and her hands crept up to encircle his neck. Before he thought better of it, Thomas wrapped his arms around her waist and pulled her against him, bending to kiss her. God, she tasted good. And when she drew away, he was shaking. Why the hell was he shaking?

She took in a shuddering breath, released it slowly. "Go. Go and take care of Shelly and her child." She bit her lip, lowered her eyes.

Damn but he hated to leave her. She seemed incredibly vulnerable right now, weak, tired. Kind of soft and pliable in his arms in a way that made him want to hold her right there all night long. He glanced over Janella's shoulder at a smug-looking redhead. "Take care of her, 'Genia. She's had a rough day."

"So have you by the looks of it, Thomas Duffy. But don't you worry. It isn't fatal." She winked.

Thomas fastened a forbidding expression on his face, turned and left on legs that were none too steady.

Chapter 8

"Here, drink this. It'll relax you." Eugenia pressed the tea into Janella's hand.

Janella sipped, let the flavor seep into her tongue before swallowing. The warmth spread down her throat and through her stomach.

"You know I'm your friend, Janella. You *do* know that, don't you?"

Janella met the woman's eyes and smiled. "Yes, I do. I'm grateful to have friends. More than I've ever had before. You, Thomas. Perhaps Shelly now. Even Humphrey."

Eugenia took a seat across from her. "Honey, I saw what happened just now with Thomas."

Janella lifted her gaze, met Eugenia's, prepared herself.

"You don't have to tell me if you don't want to, hon. But I'm gonna burst if you don't."

Janella shook her head. "There is really nothing to tell. I... I was moved by what he did." She spoke slowly, giving her words a lot of thought. She didn't want to lie to her new friend, but she couldn't quite bring herself to tell the truth, either. That she was deeply in love with a man who could never return her feelings. That she'd tried to believe he was as cold and heartless as the people she'd run away from, but that she'd seen undeniable proof tonight that he was just the opposite. "He's a special man, isn't he?"

"Yes, that he is. Though he's too dense to realize it."

Janella shrugged, unsure how to respond.

Eugenia smiled, nodding in quick, sharp movements. "Well, hon, I'll tell you something. I don't have to be a mind reader to see what's going on with you and Thomas."

Janella closed her eyes. She'd kissed him. He'd kissed her back. But she knew it was little more than the overwrought emotions of what they'd just shared that had caused his reactions.

Her own, well, they were caused by something much deeper. Something bigger and more frightening than anything she'd ever felt in her life. She leaned her head back against the sofa and sighed as she called to mind the feel of his lips on hers. The way his strong arms had run tight over the small of her back. The way his hard body pressed to hers and the feel of his hair tangling around her fingers.

But he wanted her to leave him. How could he kiss her that way if he wanted her to leave him?

"You love him, don't you?"

She felt a warm tear slip over her cheek. But she said nothing. She was so tired. The effort of sharing Shelly's pain and the act of sending her own strength into the other woman's body had left her drained and nearly limp. She lowered her head to the sofa pillow, hugging it to her face, closing her eyes.

Then softness, warmth covered her. Eugenia had taken the blanket from the sofa's back and laid it gently over her.

"That's it, you just rest now. And don't worry, hon. This is all gonna work itself out. You'll see."

Two o'clock in the morning.

Thomas carried Janella upstairs, laid her on the bed, pulled blankets over her and cursed himself for being a hundred kinds of fool. Damn, he wanted her so much he could barely look at her without getting aroused. And he could have dealt with that if that was *all* there was to it. But it wasn't. Something was happening here, and he did not like it one damn bit.

Fortunately, there was plenty to do to keep him busy for what was left of the night. Good thing, because if he hung around here, he'd probably wind up slipping under those blankets beside her. He'd never sleep anyway. What he needed was physical exertion and lots of it. He thanked the fates that the farmer who rented the land from him kept some of his equipment out in the barn, rather than hauling it back and forth. There was a tractor and a set of four-bottom plows. He hoped the John Deere's headlights were in working order as he headed out of the house.

* * *

Halloway had one of his counterparts place the call, since Janella might recognize his voice. He didn't really give a damn whether she was in this country illegally or not, and calling Immigration would be detrimental. If she was what he thought she was, then the last thing he wanted was to reveal her presence to anyone else. And he didn't want another government agency getting tangled up in this. He just wanted to know for sure before he let anything slip. He figured the more he could shake her up, the better the chance she'd reveal something. And she'd probably shake much more easily being called first thing in the morning, before she'd even dressed or eaten. Scaring women's socks off wasn't something Halloway liked doing, but it was necessary in this case. He couldn't really see any other way to get at the truth. So he sat and waited for the call to go through, hoping she'd drop a clue, tell him something.

If there was anything to tell.

Halloway listened on the extension, his lips thinning at the fear in Janella's voice as Parks—his tone intimidating as hell—identified himself as an officer of the U.S. Department of Immigration and Naturalization and began barking questions.

Thomas not only plowed the secret meadow hidden within the woods, but dragged it, fertilized it and seeded it down with winter millet. And he didn't only do the spot where the ship had disintegrated. That would have been too obvious. He did the entire meadow, which was at least an acre and a half in size.

He returned to the house cold, dirty and exhausted, besides being glad it was Sunday and he had no clinic hours today.

Janella stood in the living room, staring down at the telephone and wringing her hands. She looked as though someone had just dropped a bomb in her backyard. Thomas went to her, forgetting all about his decision not to give a damn.

She glanced up quickly, almost fearfully, relaxing only when she saw who was there. Then she closed her eyes tight.

"What is it? What's happened?"

Biting her lower lip, she faced him. "There was a telephone call... from your Immigration Department."

"Ah, damn—"

"Thomas, the man asked so many questions. He wants to know when we were married, and where, and by whom. And when we will hold the... the *ceremony* here in the United States, and... You never should have told them I was your wife, Thomas." She pushed her hands through her hair, turning in a little circle. "I'm so afraid. What are we going to do?"

Thomas looked at her, the tears streaming over her face and burning holes through his iron wall as if they were made of sulfuric acid. He caught hold of her upper arms and pulled her to him, stroked her back.

A throat cleared and Thomas whirled, still holding her, to see Alex Vrooman standing in the kitchen.

"You have two choices, Janella. Neither is a perfect solution, but both might work."

She lifted her head, stepping away from Thomas to stare at the man. "Tell me what they are," she whispered, eyes seemingly afraid of what she was about to hear.

"One is to come away with me. Right now, today. We'll hole up somewhere safe until Halloway gives up searching for you and then go on to some of your people living here in this country."

Janella blinked twice, glancing up at Thomas as if waiting for him to say something, voice an opinion. But he didn't. Instead he just swallowed hard and asked, "What's the other option?"

Vrooman shrugged. "Fairly obvious, Thomas. Marry her."

He flinched as if he'd been slapped.

Janella stepped farther away from him, head bowed. "Then there's really no choice to be made." She closed her eyes, bit her lip. "I will go upstairs now and gather my things. I can be ready in a few minutes, Mr. Vrooman."

"It's 'Alex,'" he said softly. "Take your time, Janella. I have to make a few phone calls, and—"

"Now, wait just one damned minute here."

Janella froze, her back to him. Alex's brows lifted, and he stopped speaking. The screen door creaked, and Eugenia popped in, smiling at Thomas, then staring in mute surprise at Alex Vrooman. She held a basket of bran muffins in one hand, and the other rose to smooth her hair.

Her confused gaze went to Thomas again. "What's going on? Why's everyone so tense?"

Thomas held up a hand to her for silence, turned to Janella, one hand going to her shoulder. "Look, if you take off with this guy, Halloway will be sure his suspicions about you were right. He'll probably never stop looking for you. You wouldn't have any peace for the rest of your life."

"Halloway is looking for Janella?" Eugenia cried. "Why didn't someone tell me this? Sakes alive, he was in my shop just the other day asking questions and—"

"'Genia, please." Thomas squeezed Janella's shoulder softly. "Look, why don't we just go ahead and do it?"

Janella turned slowly, blinking up at him. "You told me you didn't want a wife, Thomas. You said you would never marry."

"Exactly. So it isn't as if marrying you would be keeping me from anything. And it would get Halloway and Immigration off your back."

Her brows drew upward. She shook her head slowly.

"It won't be a big deal, Janella. A quick simple ceremony at the town justice's office. Then you just keep living here like you've been doing. Nothing will change. When Halloway gives up and goes away, you can move on to wherever you want to, and I can—"

Something whacked him in the back of the head and Thomas turned in time to see Eugenia winding up to peg him with another bran muffin from the basket. "Thomas Allan Duffy, I've never in my life known a man as downright *stupid* as you!" She practically screamed the words at him and let fly with the second muffin. He ducked it, but not by much.

"What the hell is that for?" Thomas scowled at her. "This is between Janella and me, Eugenia. Why don't you and Alex here step outside for five minutes, huh?"

"It isn't necessary," Janella said, her voice rougher than sandpaper.

Thomas looked at her, and the hurt he saw in her eyes almost knocked him over.

"Thank you for your generous offer, Thomas. It's kind to be so self-sacrificing for me, but I think I've put you to enough trouble already." She glanced at Vrooman. "Would it be all right if we left tomorrow night instead of today? I'm very tired right now. And I want a chance to say goodbye to my friends and to see Shelly's little baby girl before I go."

Vrooman smiled kindly at her, nodding. She fled then. Really ran, up the stairs, and Thomas heard the bedroom door slam.

"Well, Einstein, you've got about thirty-six hours to get it right. Think you can figure it out by then?"

Thomas closed his eyes, wondering why the hell he felt like punching someone. Preferably Eugenia.

'Genia faced Alex Vrooman and smiled sweetly. "Eugenia Overton. I don't believe I've had the pleasure."

"Alex Vrooman," he replied, taking her hand and squeezing. "Miss Overton, would you care to join me in town for some breakfast? I do believe our friend here needs some time to himself."

"What our friend needs, Mr. Vrooman, is a mule to kick him in the head. But I don't suppose you have one handy."

Vrooman laughed and, tucking Eugenia's arm through his, led her out of the house.

Thomas shook his head as he watched them go. Then he started up the stairs, intending to talk some sense into Janella. She couldn't just go off with

Vrooman. They didn't even know the guy. He could be lying through his teeth, could be working hand in hand with Halloway and his goons, for all they knew. And for that matter, he didn't much like the idea of Eugenia heading out of here with him, either. She was old enough to know better than to take up with a stranger that way.

Thomas reached for the bedroom door, then paused with his hand in midair. Soft sobs, punctuated by an occasional sniffle, came from beyond the door, arrowing straight into his heart. He drew a breath, swallowed hard and tried to still the little spasm in his stomach.

Great job, you big jerk. That ought to be your specialty, making girls cry.

Thomas ignored the boy in his head and stared, unseeing, at the door. Hell, why was she crying? What had he said to make her cry?

Mentally, he went over the conversation that had taken place downstairs, but he couldn't for the life of him figure out what her problem was. He'd offered to marry her, for crying out loud. What more did she want from him?

He balled his hand into a fist, but stopped before knocking, glancing down at his dusty, sweaty clothes and changing his mind. He'd clean up first, give her some time to get over whatever the hell was wrong. Then maybe he could talk to her.

Janella tried not to be angry with Thomas as she wiped away her foolish tears and began emptying the closet of her belongings. She folded each item neatly, made small piles on the bed. She had nothing to put

them in, but she'd worry about that later. Her posses-
sions amounted to a pitifully meager display. Some
jeans and blouses, a little mound of undergarments,
the books Eugenia had given her.

As she lay the little slingshot on top of the clothing
on the bed, tears threatened to cloud her vision yet
again. She angrily blinked her eyes dry. But the image
of Thomas with Shelly's baby returned to haunt her.
Seeing him, cradling that tiny child in his strong arms,
bending over it to breathe life into it once again, made
her heart contract in her chest. He was a special man.
A caring man, with a heart full of love.

Just not for her. It wasn't his fault. She couldn't
blame him for the way he felt. He didn't want a wife.
He'd told her as much. The very act of offering to
sacrifice the life-style he held so dear only confirmed
the extent of his kindness. But she couldn't let him do
that for her. She couldn't let him, because she wanted
so much more from him than just words on a paper
document proclaiming them man and wife. And it
wouldn't be fair to let him marry her unless he knew
that, understood it. And she couldn't tell him. She
suddenly understood the reluctance of the characters
in the movies and books. The difficulty of expressing
such deep, precious feelings to another. She couldn't
do it. Especially knowing already how Thomas felt—
or rather, how he *didn't* feel—toward her.

Marrying him would be painful. Uttering vows of
love and devotion, knowing she meant every word,
would injure her in ways she'd never imagined. Hearing him utter them back, knowing he didn't mean a
word he said, would tear her into small, bleeding bits.

She glanced down at the garment in her hand, saw that it was the black scrap of a nightgown, the one Eugenia called a "teddy." She almost laughed at her own idiocy. How had she ever imagined she could win Thomas's heart simply by donning it and going to him. It was ludicrous. He simply didn't want her. It would make little difference what she wore.

He knocked only once, before the door swung open and he stood there, looking at her. She thrust the teddy underneath the nearest pile of clothes, wondering if he'd seen it.

If he had, he seemed to decide not to say anything about it. He came forward, took a seat on the edge of the bed. "Packing?"

She nodded, going back to the closet, knowing there was nothing left there.

"Janella, we have to talk about this."

She kept her back to him. "No, I don't think we do. It's better if I go."

"Better for who?"

She bit her lip, shook her head.

"Come here."

Janella turned slowly, not wanting to go to him, not wanting even to face him, but supposing she had to convince him the decision she'd made was the right one.

"Right here. Sit down. The least you can do is listen to me." He patted the mattress beside him.

Reluctantly, Janella sat.

"Now, tell me. Better for who, Janella? Not for you, I'm sure of that much. Halloway will be more suspicious than ever if you run away."

She lowered her head. "It won't matter if he can't find me."

"Yeah, but what if he can?"

She only shrugged, not knowing what to say to him.

"Janella, I don't want you to go with Vrooman. How do you know he is who he says he is? How can you be sure he's not in on this whole scheme with Halloway?"

Her head came up fast and she met his eyes. She hadn't even considered that possibility. "Do you think that's likely?"

"It might be."

She knew he wasn't lying to her. He wouldn't deliberately try to frighten her. It wasn't in him to do that.

"Is that a risk you're willing to take?" he asked.

Janella closed her eyes to escape his dark, probing ones. "I don't know."

"Well, it doesn't matter, because it's not a risk *I'm* willing to take. I want you to stay here. You're safe here, Janella."

Pain welled up in her throat, making words difficult. "I can't marry you, Thomas," she managed.

"Why not? I'm not such an ogre, am I?"

He smiled as he said it, and she couldn't help but smile back, right through the pain that clouded her soul. "No, you're not an ogre, whatever one is. You're a wonderful, special man, Thomas. And..." Her words trailed off and she lowered her eyes.

Thomas caught her chin, lifted it, made her look into his eyes. "And what?"

Stiffening her spine, Janella forced herself to answer him. "You think you don't care about people, Thomas, but you do. You have so much love inside you, so much to give, if only you would let yourself. Marrying me would be another way for you to cut yourself off from your own emotions. By marrying a woman you don't care about, you'll ruin any chance of finding a woman you could truly love."

Thomas drew a slow, even breath, closed his eyes, licked his lips. "So who said I didn't care about you? Huh?"

Janella frowned, searching his face when he opened his eyes once again.

"Look, do you think I'd have offered if I didn't give a damn?"

She shook her head slowly, wishing he'd speak clearly and not dangle bits of nothing in front of her like bait. "I don't know what to think."

"Yeah, well, I'll tell you what *I* think. I think you ought to worry about your own problems and let me worry about mine. There's no way in hell I'm going to fall for some other woman, so you can just forget about that. And like I told you downstairs, this doesn't have to be forever. Just until this thing with Halloway blows over. It isn't as if we're swearing to be together for the rest of our lives, for God's sake."

She blinked against a sudden pain in her chest and averted her eyes.

"Janella, I want to help you. Why are you so damned determined not to let me?" He stood, pushing a hand through his hair, turning to face her. His gaze swept the articles piled on the bed and paused on the stack of novels. "Is it those damned books of 'Genia's? Have they got you hoping for some romantic hero to pledge heart and soul to you on bended knee? Is that it?"

Tears filled her eyes, one hand covering the books protectively. "What would be so terrible about that, Thomas? Just because you don't want me, do you think no other man ever will?"

"You think I don't—" He bit his lip, cutting his words off without finishing them. He rolled his eyes, spun in a circle, tipped his head back as if seeking advice from the ceiling and ended up facing her again. "Janella, that crap is fiction. It isn't real. That kind of stuff just doesn't happen in the real world."

His eyes found hers, narrowed. "Ah, hell, don't start crying again. Okay, all right, maybe it does happen for some people. Just not for me." He shook his head, reaching down to brush a tear from her face. The harshness in his own and in his voice softened considerably. "The damned honest truth of it is, you'll probably have a dozen men on their knees before too long. And you probably deserve that kind of romantic bull. Look, if it comes along, I'm not going to stand in the way. Is that it? Are you afraid you'll meet Prince Charming and have to let him go because you're tied to me?"

She sniffed, pulling her face away from his touch. "Eugenia was right, Thomas. You are an idiot."

His face clouded with anger. He bent, reaching past her and scooping up the teddy she'd thought she'd hidden. He held it up in front of him. "Maybe you've already met somebody. Maybe that's why you bought this little number."

She snatched it from his hand, so furious with him she could have hit him. "I bought it for you!" She shrieked the words at him before she could think better of it. Horrified at having said it, she turned her back to him, covered her face with her hands, the teddy still dangling from one of them.

"You..."

She shook her head, not facing him. "Just go. Go away and leave me. I don't want to talk to you any more."

He said nothing. But in a moment, his hands came to rest on her shoulders, lightly, softly. "Janella, I didn't realize—"

"Get out!"

She whirled on him, eyeing the door over his shoulder and flinging it open without touching it.

He looked at her, then at the floor. "I'm sorry. Janella, I—"

She focused her energies, slamming them into his chest with as much force as she could muster. Thomas staggered backward, eyes widening. Janella stayed where she was, sending another mental thrust at him, and succeeded in shoving him out of the room. One more burst of energy slammed the door in his face.

Exhausted, Janella slumped to the bed.

Okay, he'd blown it. He'd more than blown it—he'd nuked it. But how was he supposed to know she'd been thinking—what? Just what the hell had she been thinking? About seducing him, he guessed. About getting him hot and bothered enough to take her to bed. And he supposed he should have known that. She'd told him she was curious about sex and interested in trying it out...with him, no less. But he hadn't really thought it meant anything. Damn, did she really want him? *Him?*

Maybe there was a little more to it than that, though. Must be, or she wouldn't be mad enough to skin him alive right now. Okay, he had to stop and think this through. She wanted him in bed. He'd asked her to marry him, but he'd told her it would only be make-believe. She'd gotten furious.

So it stood to reason that maybe she wanted a marriage that came with all the extras. Sex being one of them. The big question was, what else did she want? Hearts and flowers? Love, for crying out loud?

Thomas closed his eyes and battled the panic that came with the thought. Hell, he couldn't love her. Despite what she might think, he wasn't capable of it. His emotions had been shut down for too long to just wake up again and produce something that major.

He *liked* her. Hell, he wanted her, too. So badly he could barely close his eyes at night thinking about it. But not enough to want to make her his wife, not enough to give her a lifetime commitment. So what the hell was he supposed to do? March upstairs and tell her he'd be willing to sleep with her?

He had a feeling she'd probably hit him with something large, like maybe the dresser, if he did that.

Nope, he'd blown it. And he didn't have a clue what the hell to do about it. Besides, he didn't really think having sex with Janella would be the smartest move he could make.

He didn't approach her again for a couple of hours. When he did, he found her calmer. Freshly showered and dressed, brushing her damp hair. The cast she'd worn earlier was in shreds in the wastebasket. The arm looked fine, and he decided it would be better not to scold her for taking it off without checking with him first.

He approached with caution, chose his words carefully, kept any hint of emotion from his voice. "I'm going to the hospital to check on Shelly and the baby. You want to come along?"

She met his eyes, hers hesitant, wary. "Yes."

She didn't utter another word. Just walked past him, out of the room, down the stairs. It was the same in the Jeep on the way to Saint Luke's. Stony silence, no eye contact. And she sat as far from him as she could manage without actually riding outside the vehicle.

She only softened up when they were in Shelly's hospital room. There she smiled, hugging Shelly tight. And when a nurse brought the baby in and Shelly instructed her to give it to Janella, she damned near melted.

It was something seeing her like this, her eyes damp and sparkling as she held the child close to her.

"She's beautiful, Shelly," Janella said softly. "Yes, you are, little one. You're beautiful."

"I'm calling her Christine, after Hugh's mother. But her middle name is Janella. Christine Janella Connor."

Janella looked up, blinked rapidly. "Oh, Shelly, that's..." She shook her head. "I'm honored."

"You helped me, Janella. I don't know how—I'm not sure I want to know how. But you did. I don't think I could have gotten through that delivery without you. And we're both grateful."

Janella shook her head. "It was Thomas who gave her life."

"Don't think I'm not aware of that," Shelly said. "First he saves my husband and then my baby."

Thomas looked away from the affection in Shelly's eyes. It made him uncomfortable. Damn, when that baby had stopped breathing, he'd thought for a minute he'd stop, as well. The knot of fear that had gripped him at that instant had been almost crippling. A long way from the distance he prided himself on keeping between himself and his patients.

His iron wall had thinned to a sheer curtain, and even that was worn in places.

"Speaking of Hugh," he said, to change the subject. "I'd better go check on him. I'll leave you two to visit."

He did, and when he returned, it was to find Janella a little less hostile. On the way home, he braved conversation, figuring it was worth a try.

"Did you tell her you were leaving?"

Janella shook her head. "She was so happy. I didn't want to give her a reason to feel sad."

Thomas nodded. "Yeah, well, she won't be the only one to be sorry to see you go. You know that, don't you?"

"Yes. I suppose Eugenia will miss me, as well."

Thomas bit his inner cheek. He didn't suppose it had occurred to her that he might miss her himself, had it? No. Why would it have? She had herself convinced he was completely indifferent to her. And that was the way he wanted it. Wasn't it?

Janella licked her lips, seemed to be working up her courage, and finally, she faced him. "You don't know, do you, how special it is, what you do for people?"

He said nothing, just shrugged and kept driving.

"At home..." She drew a breath. "At home, they would have let little Christine die. Any child born less than perfect is allowed to die...or...or helped to die."

Thomas stared at her so long he nearly drove off the road. He couldn't believe he'd heard her right. He veered onto the shoulder in front of the diner, killed the engine and turned in his seat. "Helped...how?"

She was staring straight ahead, deep in thought. "The old and the sick, anyone deemed a burden are...euthanized. My grandfather..."

"Damn, Janella."

"They decided he was too old to live any longer. He was scheduled for the ritual. The sick are gathered together once a year. But the flawed newborns never live more than an hour. My mother didn't even fight it. But Father did. He refused to let them take his father from him. That's why we were here all those years ago. Father decided to bring Grandfather here and hoped he could live out his days in peace."

So much pain in her eyes. So much loss. Thomas wanted to pull her into his arms, hold her, kiss the pain away.

"And did he?"

Janella shook her head. "No. The trip was too much for his old heart. He died just before we landed. He's buried in your woods, near a pond. A pine tree is his marker."

Thomas swore again, but Janella went on. "I wasn't supposed to be on the ship. But I sneaked aboard and hid. I couldn't bear the thought of leaving my grandfather here alone after Father had buried him, so I ran into the woods. That's where you found me, lost and alone. Still grieving."

He couldn't stop himself from reaching out, running one hand over her satin hair. She was so beautiful, so hurt.

"I'm glad I came along on that trip, though. That time was the last I spent with my father. He was sentenced to spend the rest of his life in prison for the crime of rescuing Grandfather. I saw him only once more before he was sent away. And he told me to come here as soon as I was grown. He said I didn't belong there, with the cold, unfeeling society of my people. He said Earth was different. That emotions were acceptable here. That no one would condemn me for *feeling*."

He stared at her, shook his head slowly. "No damn wonder you ran away. God, what kind of people *are they?*"

She sniffed, staring into his eyes so deeply it hurt. "I'm not like them, Thomas. I didn't tell you this before because I was afraid you would think I was."

He offered her a smile, cupped her head between his hands. "I know you're not like them. Hell, Janella, I've never seen anyone as emotional as you are. How you ever survived there as long as you did I can't imagine." Her hair under his palms was softly erotic. She felt fragile.

"I didn't tell you this to elicit your pity, Thomas." She gently pulled free of his hands. "I only wanted to make you realize how special you are. How precious your gift of healing is to your people." She took one of his hands in hers, her fingers caressing, tracing its shape. "Here you are free to feel, to care, to be angry or hurt or happy or excited. Yet you don't use that freedom. You close your feelings away in some darkened spot inside you. You refuse to let them out. But don't you see, you can't stop them? You can't help but care about people. It's a part of who you are. You could never stand by and watch my people practice their ritual euthanasia. You would explode in anger, and rightly so. What they are is cold and unfeeling, without emotion. You are as far removed from that as it's possible to be, but you don't realize it."

He sighed hard. Her words cut to the quick. "You're right, Janella. I do have feelings." He looked at her, as she tilted her head to one side and stared back. "And I wouldn't admit it to just anybody. Thing is, I don't *want* to have them. I have to fight them, or..." He shook his head, unwilling to finish.

"Or what, Thomas?"

"Or I'll lose my mind."

"You're wrong. You'll lose your mind if you do fight them. Worse yet, Thomas, you'll lose yourself. You'll battle your emotions until you win, and then you won't be the wonderful man you are anymore. Instead, you'll become the very thing I'm running away from."

He closed his eyes as if it would shield his soul from her probing gaze. She didn't understand. She hadn't seen the suffering, the senseless death that he had. She didn't know how much it hurt to lose patient after patient, especially when you let yourself care.

But he thought he understood finally why she wanted to flee from him. "That's it, isn't it? You're afraid I'm like those people you ran away from." He sighed hard. "Hell, you're probably right."

"No."

He opened his eyes, faced her. "No?"

"No. I know you are not like them, Thomas. You're the one who doesn't know it. Haven't you been listening to me?"

He frowned, searching her face. "Then why won't you marry me?"

She closed her eyes, shook her head.

"You want me. I know that now." Her eyes flew wide, but he caught her, clasping her nape with one hand, keeping her from turning away. "Would it make any difference if I told you I want you, too?"

She shook her head, hair brushing over his knuckles. "No. Because it isn't true."

"The hell it isn't. I've wanted you since I first laid eyes on you, lady. I want you so much I think about it every time I look at you." He couldn't believe he'd just said that. But since he had . . .

He pulled her closer, lowered his head and took her mouth the way he'd been wanting to take it. Deeply, thoroughly, thinking maybe that if he couldn't convince her of it with words, then he'd have to show her his desire. But it didn't work quite the way he'd planned.

She trembled in his arms, before she sagged against him. It was good. Her lips moist and full, parting as if on their own the minute he touched them. But when he traced their shape, when he dipped inside to taste her, the sweet friction of his tongue rubbing against hers sent a lightning bolt to the tips of his toes. And then her mouth moved under his, her tongue joined in the dance, her fingers slipped through his hair. God, he was dying, drowning in her. And he didn't want to stop.

His arms wound around her, one cupping the back of her head to hold her to him, the other encircling her waist. He pressed closer, bending her back, leaning over her as a hunger like nothing he'd ever known took control of his every cell, his every thought, his every action. All he wanted was more of her, more of her taste, her soft breaths, her passionate responses. She was so small, her soft body fitting against his hard one like a delicate hand slipping into an armored gauntlet. And everything in him screamed to keep her right there, safe from all the pain and danger in the world, safe in his arms.

She moaned into his mouth, and he felt the oddest sensation in his chest. Like something shattering into a thousand glittering fragments.

The shock of that made him draw away, and he could only stare at her in mute wonder. Her wide eyes shimmered. Her tousled hair framed a face that glowed with want, and her lips trembled, pink and wet and slightly swollen. As he watched, she lifted one hand, pressed her fingertips to her lips.

Thomas closed his eyes and slid back behind the wheel. Where he should have remained to begin with. Whatever had just happened, it scared the hell out of him. He did not like it. And he liked it even less that all of a sudden, keeping her here with him had taken on more importance than drawing another breath.

"Thomas," she whispered. Her voice sounding as shaken as his entire being was.

He looked toward her, but she was staring through the windshield, and there was fear slowly eroding the desire and surprise in her eyes.

Following the direction of her gaze, Thomas saw two men sitting on a bench in front of the diner, sipping coffee from white foam cups, talking casually. As if they knew each other, maybe.

The two men were Alex Vrooman and Jack Halloway.

And Thomas felt nothing but sheer relief. What the hell was wrong with him? He ought to be furious, suspicious. Instead he was damn near giddy.

"You can't go with him, Janella."

She met his stare, bit her lower lip. "I know."

Chapter 9

Janella stiffened when they pulled into the curved, gravelly driveway of Thomas's farm. A car was there before them. A dark, four-door boat of a vehicle that seemed designed to intimidate. It looked to Janella like the ultimate harbinger of doom. And she recognized the two men inside, the ones who'd been with Jack Halloway. She saw, too, the reason they hadn't emerged from their vehicle. Humphrey stood beside it, crouched and snarling, looking as if he'd like to make a meal of them both.

Thomas reached across the space between them and closed his hand around hers. "There's nothing left out there for them to find. They can't hurt you, Janella."

She swallowed hard, secretly finding strength in the reassuring grip, the steady voice, the honest gaze. Wasn't it enough to care so much for the man as to hurt when he hurt and laugh when he was happy? Did

she have to become dependent on him, as well? Was
that a part of this love thing? She wasn't sure, having
never experienced it before.

Thomas opened his door and got out. Janella did
likewise, catching up with him, trying to mimic the
confidence he exuded as he strode toward the dark car.
He called to Humphrey and the dog bounded toward
him, and if dogs could smile, Janella felt this one was
right now. He looked proud of his day's work.

Thomas snagged hold of his collar, and only then
did the two men emerge from the car. Halloway wasn't
with them, of course. She *knew* where Halloway was,
and with whom he was chatting.

"Well, boys, I assume you've brought your search
warrant with you this time around?"

One of the men stepped forward, wordlessly tugging a folded document from somewhere inside his
jacket and thrusting it at Thomas. Humphrey lunged
upward, jaws snapping in the air just below the man's
hand. He jumped back a little, but Thomas kept hold
of the dog.

Thomas unfolded the paper slowly, perusing the
words written there as calmly as if he were reading his
daily newspaper. Then he shrugged. "Knock your-
selves out, then. Where's your fearless leader?"

"He'll be joining us shortly," one of them said. The
other remained stone faced and silent.

"Well, I'd offer to help…" Thomas slipped an arm
around Janella, pulling her close to his side and dropping an adoring gaze on her face. One she knew was
false. "But we have a wedding to plan. Don't we,
honey?"

She blinked up at him, unable to force a reply. He turned her toward the house and strolled casually away from the two as if he hadn't a care in the world, pulling an unwilling Humphrey along with them. Janella suddenly felt as if she were carrying a very heavy weight on her back.

Eugenia flipped the pages of the *Autumn Bride Catalogue,* chattering on and on about the advantages of each gown depicted and telling Janella how beautiful she would look in any of them.

Humphrey sat at Janella's side, tilting his head this way and that, almost as if listening to every word. Janella tried to drum up as much interest as the dog. The dresses were truly lovely. But it seemed so hard to pretend excitement over a ceremony that wasn't going to mean anything at all.

"Oooh, hon, look at this one. All that lace, and the pearls worked into the trim. It's perfect for you."

Janella gazed at the photograph, forced a smile. "It's lovely."

Eugenia frowned at her, shoving the catalogue aside. "You're not very excited about this, are you?" Humphrey looked at Eugenia.

"Of course I am." The dog's head swung back to Janella.

"No, you're not. Don't you lie to me. And who can blame you anyway, with the proposal that fool of a man offered you? Just to get Immigration off your back, wasn't that what he said? I swear, sometimes I wonder how anyone that dense ever made it through medical school." Humphrey barked as if in agreement and lifted one paw to Janella's lap. She stroked his shaggy head.

"Thomas is brilliant, Eugenia. You saw him take care of Shelly's baby—"

"Brilliant about some things. But he's no brighter than a twenty-five-watt bulb about others." Eugenia's hand crept across the table to cover Janella's. "He cares about you, though. It's in his eyes every time he looks at you. He just doesn't realize it yet, or maybe he just won't admit it. Either way, you and I know how he feels. Don't we?"

Janella averted her eyes.

"You do know how he feels, don't you, Janella? Hon, you must, or you wouldn't have agreed to marry him." The woman's eyes narrowed as she perused Janella's face. "For God's sake, girl, I can't believe it. You're as thick skulled as he is." She shook her head. "You two will be the death of me for sure."

"I like the last dress the best, Eugenia." It was a sad attempt at changing the subject, but it was the best Janella could manage at the moment.

"Well, I'll order it, then. And since you have so little interest in this blessed event, I'll take care of the flowers and the reception, as well. Almost like having a daughter of my own, although I daresay if I'd raised you, you'd be a little quicker on the uptake than you are."

Janella licked her lips. "All this is going to cost a lot of..." She searched for the word. "Money," she finally added. "I don't have—"

"Girl, Thomas is the only MD in fifty miles. He has more money than God, and not one thing to spend it on. Don't you worry about money."

Janella shook her head. "I don't think—"

"Spend what you have to, 'Genia." Thomas stepped into the kitchen and poured himself a cup of coffee. Humphrey bounded up to him, butting Thomas's leg and making him slosh coffee on his hand. He scowled at the dog, but patted his head. "Just as long as we can have the wedding within a week."

"A week?"

Thomas sipped from the steaming mug. "Sooner if possible."

"You're both completely insane," Eugenia spluttered, scraping her chair away from the table and getting to her feet. "I better get busy, then. Lord, I don't know what to do with you two."

She hurried out of the house, still muttering, and Thomas glanced down at Janella and smiled. "Nervous?"

She tried to meet his eyes, only to find she couldn't hold his gaze. "This is all happening very quickly, Thomas. I never said I would marry you."

"You agreed you couldn't take off with Vrooman. I thought marrying me was the only other option."

She felt trapped, and suddenly the thought of just leaving all of them, Vrooman, Thomas, Halloway, this entire town, flitted through her mind like an errant breeze. It was enticing, the idea of being alone, free to do as she chose without worrying about the consequences.

Thomas came closer, took a chair beside her. Humphrey padded over to lie down on top of Thomas's feet. "It's gonna be all right, Janella. I promise. Don't look so afraid."

She couldn't help it. She *was* afraid.

* * *

The entire banister was entwined with red roses and
baby's breath. More floral arrangements dotted the
living room, which had been cleared of all its furni-
ture and filled with folding chairs borrowed from the
local grange hall. Lots of frills, and the scent made
Thomas want to sneeze, but he figured Janella would
like it. And hell, she deserved a nice wedding, even if
it wasn't a real one.

She hadn't talked about leaving again. Actually, she
hadn't talked about much of anything at all. She'd
become quiet, oddly withdrawn, and she avoided him
as much as was humanly possible, going to bed early
every night, saying she didn't feel like going into the
clinic with him days. He hadn't liked leaving her at
home alone, but she hadn't given him much choice.

He hadn't kissed her again. She'd shown no indication that she might want him to. And he wasn't sure
what to expect after the wedding. Did she still want to
sleep with him, or had she changed her mind? He'd
have given his eyeteeth to know what was going on in
that head of hers. Especially today.

He hadn't seen her at all. Eugenia had shown up at
the crack of dawn and kept him away from the bedroom where she and Janella had taken up residence.
He'd hoped to talk to her before the main event, to
reassure her, to ease her fears, whatever the hell they
might be. But he hadn't had the opportunity, and now
he didn't really know what to expect.

Half the town had shown up for this thing. The living room was filled to capacity and then some, with
Halloway sitting in the back, watching everything with
interest. Especially Eugenia. He seemed as fascinated

by her as Vrooman. And Thomas got the feeling 'Genia was enjoying every minute of it. Thomas was surprised the guy hadn't given up and gone away by now, having found nothing unusual out in the woods. He'd been half hoping for that, and half dreading it. With Halloway gone, Janella wouldn't be forced to go through with this scam. And for some reason, Thomas wasn't altogether sure that was what he wanted.

Stupid.

Bess Longworth, the church organist, struck up the wedding march on the portable keyboard, and the room went silent. Thomas tugged at the collar of the tux Eugenia had insisted he wear, and looked up to the top of the stairs just as Janella appeared there. And then he couldn't look away.

My God. He blinked and swallowed, and his stomach turned over. His throat clenched as she slowly descended the stairs. She was enough to send every man in the room into immediate cardiac arrest. Her hair all caught up in the back, with ebony ringlets cascading down around her face and brushing her bare shoulders. Her eyes mysterious as ever, more so with the touch of makeup Eugenia had artfully applied. The white gown revealed a hint of cleavage, peeping out from behind pearls and lace. It hugged her waist and slender hips and legs all the way to the floor, where it pooled around her feet.

But her eyes were downcast, and she wasn't smiling. She didn't look at him, just came toward him to a chorus of oohs and ahs and breathy sighs. Thomas figured some of the folks who'd shown up out of sheer curiosity were now glad they'd come. It wasn't every day they got to see a woman like Janella. Decked out the way she was, she looked like some pagan goddess. And damned if every eye that turned toward her didn't have a reverent awe glimmering within.

God almighty, this woman was marrying him. *Him*. Hell, no wonder she'd had second thoughts. She deserved one of those romantic heroes in those damned books of Eugenia's. What the hell was he thinking of, pushing her into this sham? She ought to have more, more than he could ever give her. And why it had taken him this long to realize that was beyond his comprehension.

She stopped beside him and finally looked up. He saw the tears shimmering on her lashes, and felt like the biggest idiot in the universe. He'd taken this whole thing as if it were a game, a little round of cat and mouse with Halloway. But it meant more than that, no matter what he called it. And he thought it had meant more to her right from the start. And *that* was why she'd become so depressed and so distant.

He reached down, took her hands in his and lifted them to his lips. Hell, she was hurting. This damn wedding was tearing her apart. Why couldn't he have seen it earlier?

"We are gathered here today," the Reverend Phelps began, and Thomas knew he ought to look at the man, pay attention to what was being said, but he couldn't take his eyes away from Janella's. They held him like magnets, clung to him as if she were too afraid to look away.

And then he was repeating his vows. Then she was repeating hers, and damned if those tears didn't spill over and splash down onto the backs of his hands, still clinging to hers.

He slipped his ring onto her finger. He hadn't bought her a diamond. She deserved a rock the size of Texas, and he hadn't even thought about it. Damn, if he didn't burn in hell someday—there was no justice in the world. Why'd she have to fall into his backyard? Why couldn't she have landed in the lap of some Prince Charming who could give her what she wanted, instead of a coldhearted snake like him?

"You may kiss the bride."

Thomas drew her close, gently, sensing her fragile state, wanting only to reassure her. He lowered his head and kissed her for the first time in days, and it was as if he'd crossed a desert looking for water, and instead had found champagne. So he drank, and tasted salty tears, and he felt lower than Satan himself.

The room broke into a chorus of raucous cheers. Must have been the tears that did it. First her stunning beauty, her downcast eyes, her palpable uncertainty, and then her tears. They'd worked their magic. Every busybody here suddenly felt a personal stake in her happiness. Even the women who'd shown up with daggers in their eyes were sniffling and dabbing at their cheeks, and smiling those dopey, sugary smiles that women smile at weddings and births.

Eugenia was bawling like a motherless calf. When he lifted his head, Thomas held Janella to his chest, encircling her with his arms, feeling her tremble.

"I'm sorry," he whispered into her hair. It was all he could think of to say, and he knew, too well, that it wasn't enough.

The crowd filtered outside, where a couple of awnings and a half-dozen tables and enough food for the

U.S. Cavalry had been set up. Crepe paper and balloons fluttered in the warm autumn breeze. The sky was blue and cloudless, and the air smelled like apples and fresh-cut wheat and new-mown grass. White table cloths, held in place underneath with a little masking tape, billowed in the breeze all the same. A big fat paper bell rolled over and over, traversing the length of one table to plop gently to the ground.

On a small round table in the center of it all rested an immaculate wedding cake that might have been decorated by pixies, so tiny and precise were the flowers and the trim. Someone hustled him toward it, and someone else began snapping pictures. But Thomas was barely aware of the bustle around him. He only knew that somehow, he'd managed to hurt this small, exotic woman today. And he knew that somehow, he had to make it right.

At last they were leaving. Janella hadn't thought they ever would. A few lagged behind. Eugenia and a pair of teenagers she'd pressed into service busily covered dishes with plastic wrap and stashed them in the refrigerator. Janella had changed from the beautiful white gown into a shorter, more practical dress. She wandered from table to table, gathering paper plates before the wind could disperse them. Some had already taken flight. She watched one cartwheel across the lawn and thought, that's me. Out of control. Dancing at the whim of an unpredictable wind, with no idea where I'm going. What comes next?

A hand on her shoulder made her turn. Alex Vrooman smiled gently down at her, clasped one of her hands in both of his.

"This has been difficult for you, hasn't it?"

She nodded. It was hard to believe he could be in league with Halloway when you looked up into those warm eyes. They seemed so kind.

"I'm sorry. I'm still not certain the choice you made was the best one, but I wish you happiness. Halloway seemed a little less sure of himself when he saw you crying at the altar. I was watching him."

Her fingertips went automatically to her cheeks. She hadn't wanted her tears to be witnessed by so many. But holding them back had been impossible.

"I'm going to be around for you, Janella. If you have any questions, need any help at all." He glanced past her, to where Thomas stood talking to Eugenia near the house. "Or if you change your mind."

Change her mind? She'd never really made up her mind. She looked at Thomas, and as if sensing her gaze, he glanced up. His brow furrowed and he strode toward them, leaving Eugenia to continue buzzing the lawn like a frantic little bee.

"Anything wrong here?"

"No." She said it softly. Speaking loud seemed to be an effort not worth making.

"I was going to come over and have a word with you, Thomas. I want you to know, I think Halloway was convinced. The ceremony... well, it was moving. He couldn't help but be affected by it."

"You'd know, wouldn't you, Vrooman?"

Alex tilted his head to one side, his face puckering in thought. "Thomas?" No response. Alex frowned harder, his gaze jumping from Thomas's to Janella's. "I get the feeling I've just been accused of something."

"Thomas and I saw you talking to Halloway in town the other day," she told him.

His brows went up. One hand cupped his chin and he nodded. "I see. So you decided I might be working with Halloway. Hence you couldn't leave here with me, leaving you no choice but to marry Thomas." He looked away from her, pinning Thomas with a glare that seemed to darken and throw off sparks. "That was the weakest and possibly the lowest ploy I've ever heard of, Duffy."

"What?"

She thought she might need to step between them when Thomas leaned forward. Instead, she gripped his arm, felt the tension in the bulging muscles, and saw that his hand had become a fist.

"You heard me. Did you even consider coming to me? Asking me about this? No. You used it to plant doubt in Janella's mind, and you used *that* to make her marry you."

"You cocky little bastard, I oughtta—"

"Stop!" She did get between them now, both hands bracing Thomas's shoulders. Twisting her head, she spoke to Alex. "It isn't like that. Thomas didn't *want* to marry me. He only did it because he felt he had no choice!"

"Oh, he had a choice, Janella. You're fooling yourself about that." His eyes glittered as he stared at Thomas. "You got the best of both worlds, didn't you? You get to keep her, without an ounce of emotional risk. Not a word of commitment. Not a hint of feeling. But that's the way you like things, isn't it?"

Thomas's hands rose to close on Janella's shoulders, and gently, but firmly, he moved her aside. "Go inside and help Eugenia."

She shook her head. "No. You mustn't fight over this. It's all just a misunderstanding. Thomas, please, I can't stand any more today. I—" She broke off, blinking, realizing just how close to the emotional limit she'd been pushed. Tired of all of it, she turned away. Let them beat each other bloody, for all she cared. She'd had enough.

"Look at her, Thomas. Look at what you're doing to her."

"*I* didn't do anything to her." But she felt his eyes on her back as she walked away. She tried not to slump so much, tried not to drag her feet over the grass.

"You could have found another way to convince her to stay. You didn't have to make her doubt me."

"Dammit, Vrooman, *I* doubt you. What the hell were you doing with Halloway in the first place?"

"Pumping him for information. And if you'd given it any thought at all, you'd have guessed that on your own."

Janella stopped walking. She sank down onto a folding chair, close enough to still be able to hear them, watch them. She felt badly for having misjudged Alex.

Thomas was shaking his head. "Look, if I jumped to the wrong conclusions, I'm sorry. But you have to know I couldn't risk her that way."

"You could have given her the facts and let her make her own decision, though. But I think you didn't want to do it, and I think the only risk you were concerned with was your own risk of losing her."

"Dammit, Vrooman, you're skating on thin ice."

"So I am. And so are you. I'm staying in Sumac, Thomas. I'll be here for her if she needs me, and if she decides to leave with me, go to meet others like her, then I'll take her. Don't think I won't."

Thomas looked toward her and Janella hastily averted her eyes.

Vrooman sighed hard. "Halloway's half-convinced. Soon he'll give up and go away, and Janella's reason for staying with you will go with him. Personally, I hope she will decide to come with me. It would be the best thing for her, Thomas."

With that, Vrooman walked past Thomas toward the house, calling for Eugenia. He'd driven her here this morning, then left and come back in time for the ceremony. It looked as if they'd be leaving together, as well.

Janella gathered up the trash bag she'd been filling with paper plates and carried it toward the trash cans behind the house. She didn't look back at Thomas, but she knew he was staring at her. As she removed the lid from one of the cans and stuffed the bag inside, Alex Vrooman's accusations rang in her ears. Alex might think Thomas's alleged deception would make her angry, make her want to leave. But he was wrong. She would have loved to believe it was true. She'd have loved to think that Thomas had wanted her to stay so badly that he'd used Alex's talk with Halloway to influence her decision.

But she didn't believe it. He didn't want her here. Didn't want a wife, especially her.

* * *

The chairs had been removed. Someone, probably Matthew Connor and a few of his brothers, had restored the living room to its original status. Except for the roses. There were still roses all over the damned place. He ought to have knocked Vrooman on his butt for saying the things he had. Would have, if there hadn't been just a grain of truth to them.

Thomas sank onto the sofa, pushed one hand through his hair, closed his eyes. Hell, he supposed he might as well face it. He didn't want Janella to leave. He'd danced around it for days now, but ignoring it and denying it didn't make it go away. He'd gotten attached to her somehow. Gotten used to having her around the house. And he liked it.

So what? It didn't mean a damn thing. Nothing. And he wouldn't let it start to mean anything, either. Because Vrooman was right about something else, too. Halloway was less certain than before. Soon he'd be convinced, and then he'd leave. After that, Thomas imagined Janella would be out of here like a shot. And it wouldn't be long now, either.

So Thomas figured his best course of action was to continue as they'd been this past week. Polite, but separate. No more sitting up all night watching her watch movies, laughing at the pleasure she took in them, feeling as if he were enjoying them more than he ever had. No more singing along to *Beauty and the Beast* and cracking up when he forgot the words and made up his own. No more taking her to the office with him and watching the awe and wonder on her face as he worked with the patients, the damned teary-

eyed emotions she felt for every sick kid who came
through the clinic door.

And *absolutely* no more slipping into her bedroom
at night, to just stand there and watch her sleep. No.
No more of that.

She was upstairs now. Maybe asleep already—he
didn't know. He'd heard the shower, heard the hair
dryer. Her little feet moving back and forth overhead. The gentle creak of the bedsprings as she'd lain
down.

He swore softly. The knock on the door sounded as
if it were swearing right back at him. Humphrey
barked and ran to the door as Thomas got up and
headed into the kitchen, wondering who the hell would
bother a man on his wedding night.

Yeah. Some wedding night.

Vrooman and Eugenia, who never seemed to leave
his side much lately, unless it was to pass the time with
Halloway. She was certainly becoming a femme fatale
these days.

"Thomas, I need a word."

Nodding, Thomas stood aside and held the screen
open.

"Outside, if you don't mind. Here on the porch. It's
such a pleasant night for it."

Thomas frowned, but there was an intense look in
Vrooman's eyes. Thomas stepped out, Humphrey beside him.

Eugenia went inside. "I'll just go visit with Janella
for a few minutes."

"She's in bed," Thomas said, having little hope that
it would deter her.

"Don't forget—" Vrooman told her, his eyes lingering on her face. "The radio."

"I won't forget. Sheesh." She released the door as she went in, letting it bang shut behind her.

Vrooman took a seat on the top step. Thomas, wondering what the hell was going on, went to sit beside him, and waited.

The man cleared his throat. "You're...uh...you're going to have to sleep with her."

Thomas surged to his feet as if shot from a cannon. At the same instant, he heard rock music blasting so loudly from the bedroom upstairs the windows rattled.

"What in hell is going on around here?"

Alex looked up at him, smiled a little crookedly. "I've been thinking about it, checking files on other cases where Halloway's been involved. He's thorough, Thomas." Alex patted the step again. Thomas sat down, waiting for him to come to the point.

"We have no way to be certain he didn't plant listening devices in the house while he was here today. With all that was going on, he certainly had opportunities."

Thomas swore. He lowered his head and rubbed his temples with his forefingers.

"He might not have. If not, though, he might be out there somewhere." He glanced toward the fields, the woods beyond them. "Perhaps with a set of high-powered binoculars. All he'd need to see was a hint that two bedrooms were being used rather than one..."

"I get your point."

"His suspicions would be refueled, perhaps stronger than ever. He'd never give up until he had proof of who Janella really is."

"Probably."

"You don't have to *do* anything—"

Thomas shot him a glance that stopped him in midsentence. "What do you think I'm gonna do, force her? Tell her it's all just to convince whoever might be watching and then take advantage? Hell, Vrooman, I'm not a frigging animal."

Vrooman's placid face never altered, nor did his studious gaze waver. "I didn't suggest anything of the sort. You're putting your own interpretations on my words. I only came here as a friend, Thomas. To warn you."

A little of Thomas's anger died. He sighed slowly, his spine relaxing. "I suppose 'Genia's inside filling Janella in on all this?"

Vrooman nodded. "Hence the radio," he said. "In case of bugs."

"Okay, then. Okay." Thomas started to rise, only to have Vrooman's surprisingly strong hand settle on his shoulder to keep him sitting.

"There's more."

Thomas braced himself, sensing this was no trivial matter. Something big was coming.

"The others ... tend to stick together. There's a community in Arizona where all but a few have settled. I ... I know them well."

"What are you working up to, Alex? Just spit it out."

"It's going to be hard for you to hear."

He stared into Thomas's eyes with apparent sympathy. The hand on his shoulder exerted a comforting pressure.

"They're good people. They take care of their own, but aren't hesitant to help anyone in need. I think..." He sighed. "Thomas, I think Janella needs to go there, to be with them. She seems to be falling into a state of depression, and it might go on. You're a doctor. You know how dangerous that can be."

Thomas nodded.

"I didn't mean to be so hard on you today. I was angry that my integrity was called into question. But I know you care for her. Want what's best for her."

"And you think leaving Iowa, heading down to Arizona to be with these people, is what's best for her, don't you?"

Vrooman's eyes never left Thomas's face as he nodded.

Thomas shrugged. "Fine. You just let me know when you think Halloway's called off the dogs."

The screen door creaked open, banged shut. Eugenia came behind them, dropped a hand to Vrooman's shoulder. "Ready to leave, Alex?"

Alex rose, using the railing to pull himself to his feet. He offered Thomas his hand. Thomas took it, shook it.

Eugenia snagged Thomas's neck with both arms and hugged him to the point of near asphyxia. Against his ear, she whispered, "Open up that heart of yours, Thomas Duffy. It's time. That girl up there is head over heels—"

He gently set her away, not able, not willing, to hear the end to that sentence. It was bull, anyway. Impossible. Stupid. And not something he wanted. Not something he'd been waiting for all his life. Not something that would fill up the empty pit where his heart used to be. Not something that would bring the hollow Tin Man he'd become back to pulsing, throbbing life. Never that.

Chapter 10

She heard his steps, slow and even, on the stairs. Her heartbeat sped up a little. Her palms dampened. She stood near the window, pretending to look out, but every cell was focused on the sounds of his approach. Traversing the hall. Now stopping outside the door.

It opened. Janella turned.

His eyes were apologetic. "It'll be okay."

She nodded, her gaze slipping inexorably to the bed she was to share with him.

"You look tired. Go ahead, lie down. I still have to shower and . . ."

His voice trailed off. So that was going to be the way of it. He'd give her a chance to fall asleep before he joined her. She supposed he thought it would be easier on her. How could he know that she wouldn't sleep at all, but only lie there, tense and wide-eyed? Alert to his every movement. Waiting. Wondering what would happen when he came to her.

She flicked off the bedroom light and crawled beneath the covers. Would he touch her? Kiss her? Hold her in his arms? She wanted him to. Wanted it so much it haunted her thoughts, had all this past week. She loved him. Wanted him. She'd told him the latter. She'd never admit the former, not unless he came to... Ah, but that was foolishness. He'd never...

She turned toward the bathroom when she heard the shower running. Her thoughts strayed to the black teddy in the closet. Should she get up, slip into it and wait for his reaction? Did she dare?

She bit her lip, shook her head. He did not want her. When was she going to accept that as the truth?

He took his time. She heard every movement, almost every breath. It seemed an eternity before he finally emerged. The amulet gleamed against his chest; like a brand proclaiming him hers. Why did he continue wearing it? He wore boxers beneath a short robe hanging open. His hair was wet and curling. He rubbed his head vigorously with a towel before coming to the bed, standing at the side, looking down at her for a long moment.

He sighed, shook his head, tugged back the covers. Shedding the robe, he slid in beside her, his damp body cool against her heated skin.

She sucked air through her teeth. "You're cold!"

"Sorry about that." He lay on his back, not so much as turning to face her. "I thought maybe you were asleep."

"I'm not."

"So I see."

Stupid conversation. Absolutely stupid. A tenseness filled the silence as she waited to see if he'd move closer, or roll toward her and slide his arms around her, or roll away from her and go to sleep, or talk some more.

"About today," he began, still lying on his back.

"What about today?"

A long, slow breath escaped him. "It wasn't exactly the wedding day young girls dream about, was it?"

"I don't know. What do your young girls dream about?"

He shook his head from side to side on his pillow. "Not that. They want to be swept off their feet by some man who can't live without them."

She nodded thoughtfully. "And you most certainly *can* live without me. Is that the point you're trying to make?"

He did turn to face her now, a frown puckering his brows. "Hell, no, that isn't the... Janella, I was trying to apologize. You seemed so melancholy today, and those tears at the altar were not tears of joy. You looked as if your heart was breaking."

She said nothing, only searched his face in the gray darkness, trying to see a sign. But as always his feelings, if he had any, were well hidden.

"The condition of my heart shouldn't be your concern."

He was quiet for a moment, lying back again, pensively staring at the ceiling. Then he said, "You're homesick, aren't you? You miss your own people."

"It's difficult to miss them, Thomas, when you act so much like them."

"What the hell is that supposed to mean?"

She refused to answer, and took her turn at searching the ceiling for the secrets of the universe.

"Alex thinks it would do you a world of good to go to Arizona to see them, be with them."

Janella blinked, a small knot of fear tightening in her stomach. "And what do you think?"

"I agree with him."

She closed her eyes against the flood of tears that burned in them. "When?"

"As soon as Halloway leaves. It won't be long. Alex thinks he's damned near convinced."

Despair was a black, clinging thing that covered your face with ugly hands and made you have to struggle to breathe. Tears spilled, and Janella was glad of the darkness. He was sending her away. He wanted her away from him this badly. Why? What had she done?

"Of course," Thomas went on, "it will take me at least a week to make arrangements for another doctor to fill in at the clinic. But no longer than that. And there's Humphrey. We'll have to find someone to—"

"Thomas?" She turned on her side, searching his face in the dimness. "You...you would come with me?"

"Yeah. Unless you'd rather—"

He stopped speaking as her arms wound around his neck and she hugged him hard. It was an impulsive act, but he responded, first by gasping in surprise and then by very gently holding her against him. He rolled a little onto his back, one arm beneath her, hand resting against her hair, the other lightly around her waist.

Her face was pillowed by his chest, and she felt the thundering strength of his heart beneath her.

The hand around her waist slipped upward, to touch her cheek. "You're crying."

"Because I thought you meant to send me away." She lifted her head, her face close to his, and searched his eyes. He *didn't* want to be rid of her after all. He would come with her if she decided to go. Perhaps he *did* feel something for her after all. Why else would he want to prolong their time together?

She restrained herself from blurting all that and considered again the question at hand. Did she want to go at all, even with Thomas at her side?

She sighed. "I'm still not sure, Thomas. I'm only beginning to become accustomed to Sumac and its people. Traveling to a new place..." She shuddered. "I'm not sure I want to go. Knowing you will be with me, though, will make the decision easier. I won't be as afraid."

He swallowed hard—she felt it the way she was lying on him. He cleared his throat. "Yeah, well, I couldn't very well send you off alone with Vrooman. Only yesterday I thought he might be one of the bad guys. I still have a kernel of doubt."

She felt her face change. Before, she was sure the love she felt for Thomas had been glowing from her very skin as she gazed into his eyes. Now her face felt frozen, expressionless. So the only reason he'd volunteered to accompany her was his lack of trust in Alex Vrooman.

Slowly she drew away from him. She rolled onto her side, putting her back to him, and huddled beneath the covers as a shiver worked through her from head to toe.

Dammit, he'd hurt her again. Might as well have slapped her as say what he had just said. But what the hell else could he have done? She'd been lying on top of his bare chest, wearing nothing but a whisper-thin nightgown, her hair tumbling down to tickle his skin, her scent tying him up in knots. And the look in her eyes! My God, it had shaken Thomas right to the marrow.

One more second, one more of those hot little breaths wafting over his skin, and he'd have pulled her harder to his chest. He'd have kissed her breath away, and then he'd have rolled her over, covered her body with his own and made her his wife in every sense of the word.

His wife.

The words echoed through his mind like a shot in a canyon. She wasn't his wife. Not really. And he damned well better not start thinking of her as if she were, because he didn't love her. And she deserved to be loved.

Of course, he'd lied about still suspecting Vrooman, and he supposed that if Vrooman knew it, Thomas would probably get a taste of the man's knuckles. Deservedly. Thomas didn't know why the hell he'd suddenly decided to go to Arizona with her. Maybe he was *already* getting a little too attached to her. He knew the idea of just saying adios someday soon and watching her get into Vrooman's car and ride away, not expecting ever to see her again, was more than he could do.

Didn't mean anything, though. Nothing much, anyway. Hell, she was a friend, right? As well as a patient.

Good one, Thomas. Duty to your patient. Excellent excuse and absolute bull.

All he wanted to do was make sure she got where she was going safely, got settled in, had everything she needed. What was so criminal about that?

And then say adios, and leave her behind. Right?

He closed his eyes. Hell, she might decide not to go at all, and even if she did, maybe she wouldn't want to stay there. She might visit these people and make a few friends and still want to come back to Iowa with him. It was possible, wasn't it?

Why the hell would she want to come back here? For what? What does she have here?

Friends, Thomas reasoned. She has friends, like Eugenia, and Shelly and the new baby. She won't want to leave them.

And you, right, Duffy? Her loving husband and her happy home. Wouldn't want to toss all that aside, would she? Wouldn't want to go out and find herself a real husband and a real life, when she has this perfectly good make-believe one waiting for her.

Shut up, Thomas thought. He thought it loudly, angrily, made it a mental shout. And the voice in his mind quieted. But what it had said lingered all night long.

At least, it did until he slept. And he knew beyond any doubt he had slept, when he woke up to find himself twined around Janella like a some kind of clinging vine. His lower arm pillowed her head. His upper one held her face so tightly to his chest he wondered how she breathed. One of his legs had pinioned her to the bed. As if—okay, he might as well admit it. He wasn't an idiot, and he'd had straight A's in psychology—as if he were subconsciously trying to keep her from leaving him.

And her lips were touching his chest, her hair rubbing it. He was hard the instant he opened his eyes, or maybe he had been before he'd opened them. There wasn't a part of either of them that wasn't in direct physical contact with a part of the other one. So if she awoke, she'd feel it. And she'd know that he wanted her beyond what was normal, or sane or bearable. He extricated himself carefully, rolled away from her and, since it was still early, tried to go back to sleep.

But apparently his movement had roused her. Because a second later, she was getting out of bed with an economy of motion that said she was trying not to wake him. Good, let her think him asleep. He wasn't quite ready to look into those exotic ebony jewels of hers just yet, anyway.

He heard her pad across the floor. A dresser drawer scraped open. Then the closet door creaked. A coat hanger rattled. More soft steps. She'd gone into the bathroom. Good. But why could he still hear so clearly, and why did each sound produce a vision? Fabric brushing over skin, pooling on the floor. God.

The glass door on the tub slid open. Then closed. Water came on. Thomas rolled to face the bathroom, opening his eyes just to blot out the images dancing through his mind with the sight of the closed door.

Only it wasn't closed. It stood wide. And beyond it, through the frosted-glass tub doors, he saw her. A hazy, flesh-toned, feminine shape. Arms moving with fairylike grace, to reveal the lush mounds of her breasts. Head tipping back, face turned up to the spray. Her movements were a dance, performed behind a silk curtain, for an audience of one.

He groaned and buried his face in his hands. God, what this woman was capable of stirring in him!

To distract himself, he got up, made the bed and reached into the closet for some fresh clothes of his own. His hand brushed satin, and he went utterly still. Her wedding gown hung there like a royal princess holding court. He remembered the way she'd looked in it. Like a dream. Like a goddess. Untouchable, unattainable, and so far beyond his worth it was like...like two different worlds. He smiled crookedly, but sadly, at the analogy. His hand fell away from the satin and he glanced back to the bathroom once more. He was frighteningly close to walking in there, sliding the doors open and stepping beneath the spray with her.

Dangerous thought.

"Sorry I'm late." Alex Vrooman signaled the redhaired waitress as he settled into the booth opposite Thomas. "Eugenia's kitchen sink was stopped up, and she wasn't about to let me out of there until I'd fulfilled my promise to fix it." He laughed in that understated way he had.

Katie Corrigan pulled a pad from her apron pocket as she approached them. Thomas knew her well. She'd been in his class in junior high.

Vrooman ordered, Katie left them and Thomas continued sipping his coffee.

"You wanted to talk about something," Vrooman began. "I assume it has to do with Janella."

Thomas nodded, setting his cup down. "We talked it over last night. She's not sure she wants to go. But if she does, I'm going with her."

Alex blinked, obviously surprised. "Do you think that's wise, Thomas?"

"I've given it a lot of thought. Seems to me the best possible way to do it. For one thing, it's gonna look strange for a brand-new bride to take a trip without her husband so soon after the wedding. If I go along, no one's gonna raise an eyebrow. Might be a slightly delayed honeymoon for all anyone will know. Besides, there's always a chance Halloway will follow her there."

Vrooman pursed his lips, nodding slowly. His sandwich arrived and he took a bite, not speaking for a long time, just thinking, and Thomas knew he was going to disagree.

"Go on, tell me your objections."

Vrooman swallowed, nodded. "I have only one."

"From the look on your face, I'd say it's a doozer."

He cleared his throat, wiping crumbs from his mouth with a paper napkin. "Thomas, she's going to have a chance to find her own life. She's going to find an entire community of people like her, who understand her, who'll take to her like family. And I think she's going to want to stay with them."

"I'm aware that's a possibility."

"Good. Glad to see you're not blind to it. The thing is, your presence there is likely to influence her decision. She may feel pressured to come back here with you, whether it's what she truly wants or not."

"I won't try to push her."

"You won't have to try. Just being there—"

"There's another point, Vrooman. The most important one, the way I see it."

Vrooman met Thomas's eyes, his own sincere and not a bit hostile. "Go on."

"Janella wants me to go with her."

A sigh escaped Vrooman's lips. "Well, I guess you're right. What she wants has to be our highest priority. So, you'll come along, then."

Thomas relaxed in his seat, his muscles slowly uncurling. He'd expected Vrooman to argue harder than he had. He'd been prepared to argue till he was blue in the face. He hadn't had to.

"But don't get your hopes up, Thomas. It's a close-knit community. She's going to fit right in with them, and I'm convinced she'll want to stay."

"If she wants to stay, Vrooman, then that's what I want for her."

Vrooman nodded, but Thomas could see the doubt in his eyes.

"So prepare me, Vrooman. Tell me a little about these people. What are they like?"

Vrooman leaned back against the vinyl booth seat and smiled. "In a word, they're emotional. Very feeling, caring, loving and a bit highly strung. They're exceptions to the norm on their planet. There the acceptable mode of behavior is coldness. They're taught to be practical and not to allow emotions to enter into their thinking processes."

Thomas nodded. "She told me a little about that." He didn't mention the other things she'd told him.

About the ritual euthanasia, the elimination of those deemed unfit or a burden.

"I'm sure such frigidity solves some social problems. Overpopulation, for one, the need to care for the elderly or the infirm."

Thomas's head came up. Vrooman knew about that, then.

"But it's no place for a person with feelings. There's one man in Arizona, Matalin. Good friend of mine. He was sentenced to life in prison for the crime of trying to save his elderly father from execution."

Thomas felt his pulse skip to a stop for a brief space in time. When it thudded once more he could feel it in his temples. "Execution?"

"The old man had outlived his usefulness, according to the ruling house. They get rid of their elderly by lethal injection, I'm told. Matalin, being emotional and a man who happened to love his father, couldn't bear the idea."

Thomas swallowed hard. "What did he do about it?"

Vrooman shrugged. "I don't know all the details. He doesn't like to talk about it. Just that he planned some elaborate rescue, only to have his father die before it could be carried out. Matalin was tried and convicted, but he escaped on the way to prison, stole a ship and came here."

"My God."

"Shocking, isn't it?"

It was shock he felt, but not at the social customs of Janella's people. It was shock at knowing that this man...Matalin...could very well be...

But no. There had to be others who'd tried to rescue loved ones from certain death, only to be forced to flee the consequences of their actions.

That was bull. The details of Matalin's story matched the tale Janella had told him. God almighty, was it possible the man was Janella's father? That he was here, on Earth?

"Is anything wrong, Thomas? You've grown rather pale."

Thomas snapped out of his thoughts, shook his head. "No. I just ... I have to go now."

As he slid out of the booth, mindlessly dropping a handful of bills on the table, Thomas knew there was no longer any question. Janella had to go to Arizona. And he'd have to find a way to convince her of it. Even though he was certain now that it would be the same as saying goodbye. And saying goodbye to Janella was going to tear him apart. God, where was his iron wall now? What had happened to his steely heart?

He sighed, long and low. It had softened, that's what. *She* had softened it. And he had a bad feeling she was about to break it.

Chapter 11

The spot where Janella and her father had buried Grandfather so long ago still seemed perfect. The little pond, just inside the edge of the woods. The towering hardwoods, the wild violets dotting the ground like a soft blanket to keep him warm. It had changed little over the years. She'd put off coming here, knowing it would renew an old pain. But now she felt a need to connect . . . with *family*.

As she sat on the ground beside the invisible grave, two deer picked their way cautiously to the water's edge and paused to drink. A bullfrog droned a monkish chant, and a breeze she could barely feel rippled the pond's surface.

"It's a shame you couldn't have lived here, Grandfather. You'd have loved it. The people . . . they're different here. They care." She closed her eyes, telling herself that the pain in her heart wasn't homesickness so much as loneliness. She couldn't miss a home she'd hated, or even her mother—its ruler—a woman who personified solid ice. She missed her grandfather. She missed her father, as well, but that pain was an old one. One that had been stamped in thick black ink like a tattoo on her soul a very long time ago. But she couldn't wish Father had acted differently. What he'd done was the only thing he could have done, being the man he was.

She tilted her head, realizing that in the same situation, Thomas would probably take the same course of action her father had, even knowing that it might cost him his freedom. In fact, there were many things about Thomas that reminded her of her father. His moodiness. His refusal—or was it inability?—to take orders. Was that why she'd come to love him so deeply? Because he reminded her of her father?

That might be part of it, she decided, but there was definitely more. She loved him for who he was. She loved the way he looked and the sound of his voice. She loved his touch, his kisses. She loved his talent for helping the sick and injured and the way he cared about them. And she loved his fondness for Humphrey. Another of his traits that reminded her of Matalin. Father had always been closer to animals than to most people.

Except for her. No one had been closer to Matalin than Janella had. Maybe because they were so much alike. Emotional and impulsive. Disgusted by the society in which they lived.

Matalin had been the only person she'd ever loved who'd loved her back. And the way things were going, maybe he'd be the only one who ever would. That knowledge made her miss him all the more. She'd have visited him in the prison colony if such a thing had been allowed. But her people would have been shocked by such a request. After all, she wasn't supposed to care, was supposed to simply forget him. She hadn't, though. And she knew he hadn't forgotten her, either. And she wondered if he thought of her often, if by some cosmic chance he might be thinking of her right now.

The thought warmed her a little, but not nearly enough. At this moment her absolute loneliness was too much to bear. And she knew why it was eating a hole in her heart, though knowing its cause did nothing to ease the pain.

Thomas wanted her to go. All week long he'd been patiently urging her to do so, and she'd come to some painful conclusions. Even though he would accompany her on this trip, she knew he expected her to stay in Arizona. He would return here without her. And she knew he was eager for that to happen. Why else had he been going on for days about all the reasons she should go? And though the knowledge pained her, she'd finally agreed. If he wanted to be rid of her so badly, she had little choice but to comply. He would unload his burden in Arizona. She felt like an unwanted pet.

The arrangements had been made in record time. Halloway and his men seemed to have melted away beneath the autumn sun. Eugenia was going to take care of Humphrey. A doctor from a neighboring county would handle the clinic. Even now, Thomas was showing him around the little building in town, filling him in on the special needs of each of his patients.

Shelly had brought the baby by today, and they'd shared a tearful goodbye. There was nothing left to do. Tonight she and Thomas and Alex Vrooman would board a plane bound for Arizona.

And at some point in the very near future, Thomas would board an airplane again, alone this time.

God, she didn't want to go.

Through tear-hazy eyes, she saw the larger deer's head come up, ears pricking forward. A second later, the white tail flew upward, as well, and both animals leaped into the woods and vanished from sight. A twig snapped behind her and she looked around to see Thomas picking his way through the trees.

He saw her, smiled, but there was something else in his eyes. Sadness, perhaps. But why? He wanted her gone, and he was getting what he wanted. And suddenly she knew exactly why she'd been thinking about her father and her grandfather so much today. It was because she was about to lose another man whom she loved desperately.

I'm losing her, he thought as he picked his way closer, and the constriction in his chest that came with the idea was becoming all too familiar. Why did it hurt so much?

"Thought I might find you out here."

She rose, and he saw the alarm in her eyes.

"It isn't time to go yet, is it?"

"No. Not yet. We still have over an hour."

"An hour."

It was a whisper, escaping as she lowered her eyes and finally closed them. He moved closer, stopped walking and scanned her beautiful face, hoping to burn it into his mind. She'd probably decide to stay with her father in Arizona. If the man Vrooman had told him about *was* her father. But he had little room for doubt. He was going to lose her, and it wouldn't be long at all now.

"You've been crying again. Been doing a lot of that lately." She had. Homesickness, he figured. And nervousness over the trip. And maybe disappointment in him. Some husband he'd turned out to be, trying every way he could think of to talk her into going away, leaving him. It had been the hardest thing he'd ever done. But he did it for more reasons than one.

All for her, though. First and foremost, there was her father. If the man was safe and sound in Arizona, then he couldn't let Janella go on believing he suffered in prison somewhere. She had to know the truth.

But there was another reason she had to go, leave him, find her own life. She was special, the most wonderful woman he'd ever had the privilege to know. She deserved to be cherished, showered with gifts and affection and... He sighed hard. And love. If he'd been capable of that emotion, he'd have lavished it on her. But he wasn't, and she needed someone who was.

Her eyes flicked open, meeting his. The dark lashes were damp and spiky, and a glistening tear hung, entangled in their sable web.

He clasped her shoulders, drew her to his chest, stroked her hair and her back. "I don't like to see you cry, Janella."

She hugged his waist. Her body seemed to go warm and fluid in his arms. Ah, damn, it was a mistake coming out here, a bigger mistake touching her this way. He'd managed to keep his hands off her this long. So why couldn't he have managed it for one more hour?

Hell, he didn't know why. He only knew it felt good holding her close, and he didn't want to let her go.

But he had to.

His hold on her slackened, but he couldn't quite convince his arms to release her. She tipped her head back, stared up into his eyes. God, she was so beautiful it hurt to look at her. Especially now. Her eyes were wide and maybe a little eager, the message in them as clear as if she'd spoken it aloud. She wanted him to kiss her, and damn him, he wanted it, too.

Maybe it was the knowledge that they had so little time left, or maybe it was just that he'd reached the end of his resistance. He'd been fighting it for so long he would have had to be superhuman to keep it up.

Or maybe it was just the look in her eyes that made him do it.

He lowered his head a little, saw her lips part in anticipation. When he lightly touched them with his, he felt them tremble. Her palms spread on his back, exerting a whisper of pressure. And he gave in to the need that was eating away at his soul. He covered her mouth with his, pressed it open wider, drove his tongue inside to devour and possess the sweetness he'd denied himself for so long. And she welcomed him with a burgeoning passion. An innocent passion, one she couldn't begin to understand. Knowing that, he shouldn't let this madness go on.

But he couldn't stop it.

His fingers tugged the blouse from her jeans, slipped beneath it to trace the shape of her back. His palms ran up the gentle curve of her spine, to her shoulders. No bra barred the way. That knowledge seared him, and he drew one hand around her, between their bodies, beneath the blouse. Her breast filled his hand, fitted it, the pebble-hard nipple poking into his palm. She drew a harsh gasp when he rubbed his rough hand over the sensitive nub. He hadn't thought it possible to want a woman the way he wanted her. But here it was, real and powerful and undeniable. He'd never felt this kind of desire in his life, and it scared him. But he couldn't turn away from it.

Or from her.

When she drew back a little he blinked in shock, letting his hands fall to his sides. Was she frightened? Was he out of line? Would she scorn him now for being a base-driven animal?

No. As he watched in silent mesmerization, her perfect hands rose to the front of the blouse, and one by one, the buttons were freed. It gaped, showing him the flat belly and taut skin he'd been unable to put from his mind. Then she shrugged the garment from her shoulders and it slid silently down her arms to fall on the ground.

Thomas felt an urge to fall on his knees in front of such ethereal beauty. But she came forward again, her nimble fingers going to his buttons this time. And in seconds she was pushing his shirt away, to join hers on the forest floor. She pressed herself against his hair-roughened chest, closed her eyes as she moved. Her hands traveled over his back and shoulders, and her lips touched his neck, his jaw, hesitated near his ear.

"I...don't know what to do..." Her innocent whisper made him bite back a groan. "Show me, Thomas. Please, just this once."

He felt a shudder rock him to the core as he bent to kiss her throat. Then he fell to his knees, ravenous for more of her, and caught one yearning nipple in his mouth. He sucked hard, working the tip with his tongue and teeth, and Janella cried out. Her knees buckled and she sagged until only his arms anchoring her waist to his chest kept her from falling. Her hands clutched his head, fingers kneading there. She was so good, so sweet. Her breasts were a forbidden fruit, her entire body his ultimate temptation. And he relished every taste, every sensation.

Mindless need tore through Thomas as he lowered her to the cushion of pale violets. His fingers shook when he released the button and lowered the zipper of her jeans. He pushed the denim and the panties beneath it down over her hips, bending over her, kissing each bit of flesh as it was revealed to him. His lips followed his hands over her thighs, her knees, her calves, right to her bare little toes. He took his time, realizing dully that he wasn't just making love to this woman. He was worshiping her, and it still didn't seem he gave her all she deserved.

When she was naked, reclining in the green-and-purple bed like a goddess, he could only kneel beside her and stare. If ever there were an illustration of perfect feminine beauty and mind-bending allure, then it was here, right in front of him, right now.

She lifted her hands toward him, and Thomas was hit with the enormity of the gift she offered. She wanted him. *Him.* What had he ever done in his lonely existence to make him worthy of this?

He lowered himself beside her, took her in his arms and kissed her mouth, his hands kneading and pinching her breasts, before slipping lower. He parted her secret folds, felt the dewy moisture they concealed, thought he'd lose his mind here today. Especially when her hands moved between their bodies to open his jeans and her palms skimmed his backside as she eagerly shoved them down.

He rolled to one side long enough to kick free of a tangle of clothing and footwear, suddenly in a hurry to be naked beside her. And when he faced her again, it was to see her gaze roving over his body, pausing on the hardness between his legs, which was so aroused it was almost painful. Timidly, her hand reached for him, fingertips touched, drew away at his harsh gasp, then returned to close around him. She squeezed experimentally, watching his face, her own eyes dark with passion. Her hands were silky soft and strong. And she ran them over him, around and beneath, lifting, squeezing, watching his face as if trying to learn what pleased him by his reactions.

He took her hand in his and moved it gently up and down, feeling the warmth of her palm stroking him. Then, biting his lip, he pulled her hand away, lowered his body gently atop hers. He kissed her again, and their tongues mated, twined and battled. With his fingers he found the core of her desire and worked it mercilessly as her breaths came fast and shallow and her hips rocked off the ground. He licked the inside of her mouth, savoring her taste as he dipped a finger inside her, then two, testing her, hoping he wouldn't hurt her, but knowing he couldn't wait much longer. She was tight, small, but so wet. For him.

Gently, he pressed her thighs open, settled himself between them, felt her juices coating the tip of him where it pressed against her. Exercising more restraint than he'd known he possessed, he nudged inside her. Just a little at a time, pausing at intervals to give her body a moment to adjust to the feel of him filling her. It was heaven and hell and ecstasy and insanity all balled into one hard knot in the pit of his stomach.

She shuddered, but never closed her eyes. They remained open, fixed unblinkingly, sparkling and black, on his. He met with the bit of tissue that offered resistance and pressed deeper. She bit her lip, her nails sinking into his shoulders the only indication she'd felt pain or discomfort.

And then he moved slowly, steadily, sheathing himself inside the damp satin that was her, pulling back, moving forward again. His gaze locked on hers, he saw the pain in her eyes recede, to be gradually replaced by acceptance and then wonder. Her lips parted as her breaths grew rapid and short. He bowed to suckle her breasts, one after the other, and her pleasure increased. He never took his gaze from hers.

He moved faster, thrust deeper, and Janella's hands curved around his backside to urge him on. She began to move with him, rocking beneath him to accept his thrusts, little whimpers of pleasure escaping her parted lips. He was at the brink, and he felt her tightening around him more and more. He took her mouth, his tongue thrusting with like rhythm, swallowing every little cry she uttered. And then she tensed, screaming his name, hands holding him deeply inside her, her body convulsing, milking him. And he held her dark gaze as she drew the essence of his body into hers, drew it from the very tips of his toes, it seemed, and tried to extract still more.

Nothing had ever felt so good. Or so right.

Every one of his muscles melted. His bones themselves turned to water and he lay on top of her thinking he never wanted to move again. A satisfaction like none he'd ever known was the result of this liaison with Janella. A sense of peace, and contentment, and fulfillment. Not to mention that he'd experienced the best damned climax he'd ever had. Shattering.

He slid off her, to the side, gathering her into his arms and wishing he never had to let her go. What was it that made this sex so different from any other? The setting? The time of day? What he'd ingested lately? Was it Janella? Was this ability to mate with a man's soul as well as his body another of her extraterrestrial abilities?

Her lips pressed to his chest, and Thomas closed his eyes.

"Thank you for that," she whispered.

She was thanking *him?* He stroked her hair, held her closer, bent to kiss her forehead. What the hell was he ever going to do without her?

"There you are. I was beginning to think you'd changed your minds."

Alex Vrooman smiled softly as he held the car door for Thomas and Janella to get in. Thomas had already transferred their luggage from the Jeep to the trunk. Alex slid behind the wheel, and Janella was surprised to see Eugenia get in the passenger side.

She turned, as if reading her mind. "I'm coming along to the airport to drive the car back. And I'll pick you up when you come home again." She blinked a dampness from her eyes and averted them. "And you *are* coming home. Don't you even think about staying with this long-lost friend of yours down in that barren desert of a place. I'll come get you myself if I have to."

Janella smiled, but knew it was a sad smile. She didn't want to leave, and she knew Thomas didn't expect her to come back. He wouldn't have made such sweet love to her in the woods today unless he knew it was safe. That she was leaving. That he wouldn't have to face her much longer and wouldn't have time to discuss what had happened between them.

For just a few moments, Janella had been certain the cold ice he kept packed around his heart had thawed. She'd felt it. He'd let himself love her, if only for those few moments there among the violets. She'd never felt so cherished in all her life, and she wished she could get that feeling back again.

But she couldn't. He'd reverted to his normal self again. If anything, he seemed more distant now than before. He calmly reminded her to fasten her safety belt as Alex pulled the car ahead. She did it, noting that with both belts fastened, they couldn't sit very close to each other. Probably the only reason he wanted them on. She wanted to be next to him, his arm around her, her head nestled in the crook of his neck. She wanted to share whispered secrets and laugh up at him the way the lovers in the movies and the young couples she'd seen in Sumac always seemed to be doing. But apparently it wasn't going to happen.

Though there was *something* different about him. He was pensive, spoke very little. He gazed out his window most of the time, unless she turned to look out hers, in which case, he would stare at her. She could feel his gaze on her, but he always averted it before she could return it. He seemed to be fighting some inner battle. Something was tearing him apart or tying him up in knots of tension. She only wished she knew what.

She knew too well what was raising chaos in her own heart. Her love for him, and now something new and unexpected. Desire. She'd heard it mentioned often in the movies, but hadn't fully understood what it meant until now. Now she could barely look at Thomas without feeling a tightening sensation in the pit of her stomach. It was like hunger, but deeper. She craved him, his body, his touch. It made her uncomfortable and restless and even a bit short-tempered. She wanted to reach for him right now, pull him to her and beg him to make love to her again.

But of course she couldn't do that.

Jack Halloway watched from a distance. A big distance. He hadn't learned a damned thing by following them or pressuring them. So he went to plan B. Give them enough rope... And sure enough, the minute they thought he was gone, they all boarded a plane for Arizona. He'd been right about Janella all along. But Vrooman was still a big question mark. Who was the man? What was his true interest in all this? Whatever his intent, Halloway had a sick feeling in the pit of his stomach that it wasn't good. So he was heading to Arizona. When they got there, he'd be waiting. But not where they could see. He'd be like a shadow.

She'd have laughed at the primitive flying machine if she hadn't been so devastated at the thought of leaving Thomas and frightened at what might lie ahead. Her fears took on a whole new ferocity when she got a look at the place. It seemed little grew in Arizona. It was brown and barren, this little airstrip in the desert. The only things that moved beneath the blistering sun above were wisps of dirty sand spiraling like ghosts and spherical tangles of some sort of weed that appeared dead, rolling at the whim of the wind. There were a few odd-shaped things growing, not trees, but vegetation of some sort, their pale-green skin coated with prickles.

They drove away from the airstrip in a car that had been waiting. Alex must have made arrangements for it. It carried them over a flat, straight ribbon of pavement that shimmered with heat.

And gradually, things became greener. A cluster of buildings rose in the distance, looking a bit more normal. And as they drew closer, she saw that through irrigation, a small city thrived in the midst of this barren land. On its outskirts, lush green lawns grew, sprinklers giving them precious moisture. Some trees and flowers thrived here, and they passed a swimming pool built into the ground, with children splashing in every available bit of water.

The houses were neat and new. Not the old over-sized homes of Sumac. One story, for the most part, with open patios and pools in the backyards, and neatly clipped grass, and nice cars in the blacktop driveways. No tractors lumbering up the winding roads or groaning through fields, though. No golden wheat fields dancing in the wind. And no hint of Sumac's cool breezes. She saw the flags some flew in front of their homes hanging limp and lifeless.

"It's really a prosperous town," Alex said softly, looking over his shoulder at her. "There are two shopping malls, a community theater. They even have their own orchestra. The main business is tourism. There are a couple of theme parks nearby, hotels, the works."

Janella shook her head, sliding closer to Thomas without thinking first. So many people. The streets were lined with cars, and bicycles and faces. The houses were closer together now, one after another. And she saw the tops of buildings in the distance, at what must be the small city's center.

Thomas's hand closed on Janella's, and she felt warmed by his touch, despite the frigid stale air that kept the car's interior cool. A tingle of longing crept over her spine, but she fought not to let it show.

"You're not trying to tell me these people are all—"

"Good God, no, Thomas. Most of them are just like you...you and me. Only about two hundred of the residents come from Janella's planet."

She blinked, staring out the side window, wondering if the boy on the bike or the man in the minivan might be her blood brothers. "How will I ever find them?"

"They'll find you, Janella. Don't worry about that. We'll get you and Thomas settled in the hotel, and I'll let word get out to one or two of them. Word will spread like you wouldn't believe, and the next thing you know you'll be overwhelmed with visitors."

She was relieved to hear that, but when she looked at Thomas, he was frowning. She ignored the urge to press her lips to his brow and smooth that frown away.

"What is it?" she whispered.

He shook his head, his mouth drawn tight. "Vrooman, I thought you knew these people personally. You said you were good friends with some of them."

"Oh, I am. But, Thomas, it's been a long time since I've been back here. And calling those I know one by one would be tedious at best, assuming I could even reach them. Besides, they tend to be a wary bunch." He shook his head, turning the car right, then waiting at a traffic light to turn left. "No, if I were to just announce that Janella was here and invite them over, they'd probably think I was another Halloway, out to trap them. I know the way they think, Thomas. Honestly, it's better just to leak a word or two and let their natural grapevine take over. In a few days, everyone will want to meet Janella."

He turned again, pulling into the curving driveway of a tall, boxy building surrounded by palm trees and exotic flowers. "Our hotel," he announced.

A young man leaned over to open Janella's door. She shot a frightened glance at Thomas.

"It's okay. Go ahead, I'll be right behind you."

She nodded and got out. Alex joined them after handing his keys to the youth. Janella saw the boy taking their luggage from the trunk. He then handed the keys to another boy, who drove the car away, presumably to park it. Alex went ahead of them to the smiling woman at the desk. "I have a reservation in the name of Vrooman and one in the name of Duffy," he told her.

Janella looked around the elegant lobby, thinking it pretty, but rather cold and impersonal. So far removed from Thomas's cozy living room. And there seemed to be strangers everywhere. Several pairs of eyes stared openly at her, and she shifted her feet uncomfortably. Why were they so interested in her? Who were they, anyway? Did they know her secret? Could they see, somehow, a sign that she was not one of them?

In seconds Vrooman had a pair of plastic cards in his hand. He handed one of them to Thomas. "Why don't you two go on up? I'm going to get things under way."

The people continued watching her, and Janella felt like crawling under the carpet on the floor to escape those knowing eyes.

Thomas took the card in one hand, clasped Janella's hand with his other and led her down a hall and into an elevator. But she felt those strange eyes on her back the whole time. The doors slid closed and she sighed in relief. They were alone.

Too much was happening too fast. An icy finger of dread traced a path over her spine and Janella knew it wasn't just her nervousness. Something was wrong. She could feel it. She glanced up at Thomas, very nearly blurting that she hated it here, that she wanted to go home, now, with him.

But she couldn't do that. He expected her to stay. If she told him how she felt, he'd take her back with him, even though he didn't want her. She couldn't force herself on him that way.

"You're scared, aren't you?" he asked, reading her feelings as if she *had* spoken them after all.

"A little."

"Don't be." He took her hand again, squeezed it gently. "I'm not going to let anything bad happen to you, Janella. I promise."

She tried to smile, but if it looked as forced as it felt, it wouldn't fool him. His reassurance was a weak one, because she knew he'd leave her soon. And then what would she do? Giving in to her fear, she slid her arms around his waist, pressed her face into his shirt.

His strong arms came around her as she'd hoped they would. Oh, if only she could stay right here, protected and safe in his embrace, forever.

But the car stopped and the doors slid open. Thomas stepped away from her, took her hand. "Come on. It'll be all right."

Chapter 12

Thomas had reserved a suite. He'd known somewhere inside him that he probably ought to get them separate rooms, but his mind had balked at the idea. He hadn't stopped to analyze that, partly because he was afraid of what that kind of soul-searching might reveal. He didn't want to figure out his motivations. He just did what felt right, and keeping Janella with him for as long as possible felt more right than anything else he could think of. So he'd booked a suite.

And it was a nice one. Roomy, with a little living room and a kitchenette separated by a hardwood counter. The bedroom was through a door on the right, bath just beyond. There was a tiny cubbyhole of a refrigerator and a little two-burner stove. A sofa and chairs, a wet bar, a TV and VCR.

Janella barely looked around, though. She just walked to the sofa and sank onto it, her eyes wide and glazed. She was scared to death. Of what, Thomas had no idea. She certainly shouldn't be this afraid of meeting some of her own people. People who'd fled their planet for the same reasons she had.

Seconds after he closed the door, someone tapped on it. The bellhop with their luggage. Thomas let him in, tipped him and closed the door behind him when he left. Janella still sat, staring at nothing.

"Try and enjoy this, Janella. Think of it as our honeymoon, okay?"

She blinked and met his eyes, and he thought he detected a glimmer in hers. Tears, maybe. So he'd said the wrong thing again. That was about par for the course, wasn't it?

He ought to tell her, he supposed, that there was a chance her father might be here. Maybe that would cheer her up. But he hesitated. If it turned out he was wrong, her devastation would be worse than ever. No. Better to wait until he was sure.

Meanwhile, he suddenly realized, he had the perfect opportunity to make up for the sham of their wedding day and the pain he'd seen in her eyes.

"So, what do you want to do first?"

She frowned. "Do?"

"Sure. We're not just going to sit here staring at the walls, are we?"

She knew what he was doing. He wanted to keep her too busy to have time to worry or feel afraid. And it worked. Thomas insisted on taking her shopping, helped her pick out a bathing suit, bought her expensive perfume after spending an hour sniffing from various bottles. They walked through the busy streets, browsing in countless shops and finally ending up at the small, but elaborate theater, where they stood in line for tickets. And then he sat beside her through a production of *The Music Man* that had her laughing and crying alternately.

Afterward, arm in arm, they walked slowly back to the hotel. And she felt good. So close to him, closer maybe than ever before. And when she leaned into his side, he didn't pull away, but instead slipped an arm around her shoulders as if it were a natural thing to do. It certainly felt natural to her. Walking at his side, in the cradle of his strong arm, beneath the pale half-moon in a starry sky.

"Enjoy the play?"

She smiled up at him. "It was wonderful. Did you?"

"Well, it's not Broadway, but it wasn't half-bad." He looked through a window as they passed it and stopped walking. "What do you say to something to eat, hmm? My stomach is empty."

She nodded. She'd have agreed to anything that would prolong this time with him. When would he leave? she wondered. How much longer would she have him near her this way?

He guided her through the doors of a small café, chose a table, even held her chair for her. He really was attentive tonight. She'd noticed that Alex had a room to himself, while she and Thomas shared one. Had Alex made those arrangements? Or had it been Thomas's idea? And if it had been Thomas, then why had he done it? The thought that he might not be averse to making love to her again niggled at her brain nonstop.

A waitress brought them menus, and Thomas excused himself while Janella perused hers, heading toward the pay phone in the back. He was calling to check in with Alex, she knew. And a chill of foreboding crawled over her spine.

"Can he be trusted?"

She stiffened as the deep whisper came from just behind her, near her ear. Turning in her seat, she came face-to-face with a young man whose hair and almond eyes were as dark as her own.

"Can he?" the man repeated.

She blinked and nodded, terror making her throat go dry.

"Who is he?"

She wet her lips with her tongue. "My... my husband."

A little of the harshness left the man's face, and he glanced toward Thomas. He nodded and stared hard at her again. "And the other one, the one who came here with you?"

She shook her head, confused and frightened. "I don't understand what you want to know."

Dark eyes narrowed, but the set jaw eased fractionally. "Your father is a hunted man, Janella. Your mother's reach is long, felt even here. We can't be too careful."

She knew her eyes widened, and she fought to breathe. "My father?"

The man nodded, his gaze darting every few seconds to Thomas across the room, his back to them. "If you want to see him, it will have to be alone. I can't be sure of the two men."

"*See* him? I don't under—"

"You must tell no one, Janella. *No one,* do you understand? Your father's life will be in jeopardy if you do."

"My *father* is serving a life sentence in prison." Her fierce whisper drew the waitress's eye. She frowned at them, a little concerned, perhaps.

The man blinked, shock erasing the insistence from his eyes. "You don't know? Honestly, you don't..." He glanced up, and Janella followed his gaze. Thomas had turned in their direction, and while he still held the phone to his ear, she knew by his frown he'd be coming over in seconds. "Your father is here, Janella. I swear it to you. He knows you're here and he wants to see you."

Thomas was hanging up the phone now. He came toward them.

"Tonight," the man said quickly. "Midnight, room 804. And come alone." He turned and hurried away, going through the café's door and out into the night just as Thomas's hand fell on her shoulder.

She jumped, startled.

"What's wrong? You're white as a sheet." He took her chin in one hand, turned her face to him. "Who was that guy? What did he say to you?"

She blinked, trying to erase the confusion from her mind. Her father? Here? Could it be?

She bit her lip against a flood of hopeful tears and shook her head. "Nothing, Thomas. Just a stranger making small talk." Lies. Lies, told boldly to the man she loved. It sickened her to utter the words. And it seemed senseless. She knew she could trust Thomas, more than anyone in the universe. She'd trust him with her life.

But if she told him, he'd insist on going there with her tonight. And if he did that, she might miss the opportunity to see her father again. She couldn't take that chance. She'd tell Thomas everything, but tomorrow, when she'd learned what this was all about.

She was keeping something from him. Thomas could see it in her eyes. And he could see, too, that she didn't like doing it. For the tenth time since they'd left the café, he wished he'd collared the jerk who'd been talking to her and demanded to know what he'd said. Whatever it was, it had upset her. He didn't like seeing her distressed. And he especially didn't like that she felt she couldn't share it with him.

She was in the bathroom now, getting ready for bed. Thomas had unpacked for both of them after she'd taken what she needed from her suitcase. Then he paced and he wondered. And worried.

Something was happening inside him. Something way down deep was stirring to life, like a big powerful dinosaur that had been asleep for a hundred years. It was coming awake in there, and it was taking control of his every thought. Thomas paced and tried to identify it. He thought it might just be the remnants of the child he'd chased away from his heart. All grown up and ready to take the reins. And though he'd fought it, the kid was winning. He'd already made up his mind to do something he hadn't thought he'd ever do.

He was going to tell Janella that he wouldn't mind if she decided to come back to Iowa with him. He was going to tell her it would be okay with him if she wanted to continue living with him, being his wife.

She'd probably turn him down cold, especially if it turned out her father was here. But he couldn't leave without at least offering. Just in case she didn't realize how he felt.

He blinked as that last thought went slinking through his mind like a criminal dodging the police. How he felt. Hell, *he* didn't even know how he felt. Except sort of bereft and black at the thought of going back there without her. Facing that big empty house again, after she'd filled it for so many days with her sunny presence, was not a prospect that appealed to him.

Okay, so he'd make the offer. And whatever she decided, it would be fine by him.

Sure you will, Thomas. You'll make the offer, and you'll put it to her just the way you've planned. But you and I both know what you want to do is ask her—no—beg her to come back home with you. But you won't do that, will you? Because you're just a big, stubborn fool.

It was the kid's voice, with the force of *T. rex* behind it, instead of the timid, soft one he'd heard inside when he'd first come back to Sumac. He mentally ordered it to shut up and leave him alone, but he had a feeling that kid was smiling smugly somewhere in there. He might shut up for the moment, but he'd be back. He'd taunt Thomas to no end if he went back to Sumac alone. Probably for the rest of his life, Thomas would hear that kid telling him what a fool he'd been to let her go.

But what the hell was he supposed to do about it?

He flung himself onto the bed, staring at the ceiling. His feelings were a mess. He didn't know what to call them or how to act on them. It was the first time he'd experienced anything like this, and for someone who'd shut his emotions off entirely for such a long time, it was nothing less than total chaos. He was confused. Where was the guy he used to be? The one who knew exactly what he wanted from life and who let nothing stand in the way of getting it?

The bathroom door opened, but he didn't turn. He couldn't look at her right now. Had to toughen himself up again first, or he'd end up blurting something stupid.

Her footsteps were barely audible as she came into the bedroom, stopped beside the bed.

"Thomas?" It was a quavering whisper.

He turned his head and looked at her, and it seemed every organ in his body stopped functioning—all but one, anyway. She stood there dressed in nothing but that black teddy. His eyes roamed every inch of her body, from her bare feet and perfect legs to the skin visible beyond that sheer black fabric. Flat belly with its dark depression in the center. Firm round breasts he could taste again just by looking at them. The slender column of her throat. And then her face. Lips parted and damp, eyes round and uncertain.

He sat up slowly and reached for her, his hand skimming over her waist until his arm encircled it, and he pulled her down onto the bed beside him. She lay on her back, staring up as if half-afraid. He was on his side, bracing himself up so he could feast his eyes on her. She was every man's fantasy come true. And again he wondered why she would want a man so unworthy of her as he was.

"If you don't want to," she whispered, "it's all right. I'll under—"

"Hush, Janella." She still seemed unsure, so he lowered his head, tasted her lips slowly, languorously, savoring every second of it.

Her fingers twisted and played in his hair as he fed on her mouth. And she kissed him back when she realized he wasn't going to reject her. God, how could she have ever thought he might?

She loved him with every breath she drew, every beat of her heart, with every cell in her body. She loved him. And she couldn't bring herself to tell him, so she showed him instead.

She undressed him, needing him so desperately it made her hands tremble, made her clumsy. When he was naked beside her, she kissed him, his mouth and his jaw, and then his wonderful broad chest. She paused when her lips touched the cool stone of the amulet, and she met his blazing eyes. "You've worn it all this time."

Thomas only nodded.

"Why?"

He shook his head as if to clear it. "I'm not sure."

"I am," she whispered before she resumed kissing his chest. He'd kept the pendant for the same reason she'd cherished the slingshot all these years—because she and Thomas were meant for one another. Somewhere inside him, Thomas must sense that. It was so sad that he'd never admit it. But maybe—tonight—she would convince him.

She worked his nipples with her mouth, remembering the way he'd done so to her and the pleasure that had rippled through her when he had. She wanted to give him that same pleasure. She wanted him to feel for her the way she felt for him.

Her lips skimmed lower, over his belly. She kissed his thighs, and then, gathering her courage, she pressed her lips to the hardness between them. He shuddered, and she knew it pleased him. She parted her lips, took him between them, worked him the same way she'd kissed him, using her tongue and teeth until he gasped her name on a voice that was ragged and hoarse.

His hands clasped her shoulders to draw her upward. She straddled him, her thighs brushing against the soft hair on his. She lay down atop him, and he held her tight, kissed her madly.

It seemed to Janella that Thomas only dropped his coldness and pretense when they made love. As she lowered herself over him, taking him inside her, she felt this was the real man, and the feelings he refused to admit to showed here and now, as they made love.

He must care for her. He must, or he wouldn't move inside her so gently. His hands wouldn't run over her body almost reverently. He wouldn't kiss her as if starved for the taste of her mouth. He wouldn't whisper her name over and over again. She knew he'd been with other women, women he hadn't cared for, but she couldn't believe he'd been this way with them. She felt cherished the way he caressed her and kissed her. Surely it hadn't been this way for him with the others. Janella felt certain no other man could make her feel the way Thomas did. It must be the same for him. It must.

Her thoughts ground to a halt as Thomas drove everything from her with the sensations he was making her feel. Wonder and joy and rapture took a back seat, for a short time, to incredible pleasure. Physical ecstasy swirled through her body like a cyclone, driving her to the pinnacle with remarkable speed.

She clung to him, panting, clutching at his shoulders. His movements slowed, gentled, but didn't stop. And as he began stroking her again, she slowly realized it was starting over.

Gathering her in his arms, Thomas rolled her over, covered her body with his own and continued showing her the wonders of physical love. When she climaxed this time, he was with her, shuddering and whispering her name as he spent himself inside her.

When it was over, he held her close, and she longed to hear him say he loved her. Or that he was fond of her. Or that he was glad they'd made love. Instead, he only kissed her eyelids and said nothing at all.

Damn him for keeping his feelings to himself. He must feel something! Joy, regret, disgust. Something! Why wouldn't he talk to her, tell her what was going through his mind?

But wasn't she doing the same thing? She knew what she felt, and yet she kept silent. Maybe she was wrong to do that. After all, one of the reasons she'd come to this planet was for the freedom to express her feelings without censure. Finding Thomas again had been the biggest reason, of course. But she was being unfair to both motivations if she refused to share what she felt with him.

So she should tell him. Mainly because she couldn't believe in his coldness any longer. She'd seen none of it here. Only tenderness and kindness and caring. And he might think himself incapable of feeling anything for her, but she didn't think he could make love to her the way he had unless he did feel something. Whatever that something was, it was enough. She was going to tell him that she didn't want to stay here. That she wanted to go back to Sumac with him, bring her father, too—if he was really here. And she thought Thomas would probably agree to let her come. He might want her to get a house of her own to live in. And she would take a job helping Eugenia at the shop to pay her rent. But whatever happened, she *knew* that in time he could learn to love her the way she loved him. She would *make him* learn to love her. She'd go to him every night and show him with her body how wonderful it could be between them. And sooner or later, he'd realize what she'd always known. That they were meant to be together. She'd begun to doubt that in the past few days. But this night with him had reaffirmed her earlier conclusion. He was meant for her and she for him. The sooner he came to understand that, the better for both of them.

She smiled as she made her decision. She touched his face with her palm. "Thomas?"

He didn't respond. She rose on one elbow and stared down at his relaxed face, his closed eyes. He was sleeping. And for a moment she just let her eyes drink their fill of his beautiful face. No worry clouding his brow. No tightness in his jaw. She wished he could be so relaxed all the time.

Her smile died as she glanced at the clock beside the bed. With a little jolt she realized it was nearly midnight. Looking at Thomas once more, she wished she didn't have to leave him. But her plan of action could wait until morning. Right now she had an appointment to keep.

Thomas slept soundly as she carefully slipped out of the bed. She retrieved the clothes she'd deliberately left in the bathroom and tiptoed into the living room to put them on. She pulled the jeans right over the teddy. Added the pretty silk blouse and brushed her tousled hair. Carrying her shoes until she got into the hallway, she slipped out. Then paused to put them on.

She was wonderful. She did things to his senses, touched parts of his soul where no one had ever ventured before. He didn't want to lose her. Dammit, he wasn't going to. He'd been dozing in the most contented sleep he could remember, when she'd slipped out of bed. The emptiness was what woke him. Well, whatever she'd got out of bed to do would be done in a second or two. She'd come back and snuggle into his arms, and if it killed him, he was going to ask her to come back to Sumac with him.

A sound made him frown and come more fully awake. Where the hell was she going?

Thomas slid out of the bed when he heard her close the hotel-room door. He yanked on his jeans and went barefoot into the next room, blinking in disbelief. Janella had crept out of here like a thief. Why? What the hell was she keeping from him? He thought immediately of the man he'd seen talking to her at the café earlier, and of how upset she'd seemed afterward. He'd known she'd been keeping things from him then, but hadn't wanted to push her. Maybe he should have.

He went to the door, pulled it open in time to see her stepping into the elevator at the end of the hall. He didn't get it. He just didn't—

"Thomas?"

He turned to see Alex Vrooman standing in the doorway of the room next to theirs. Unlike Thomas, Alex was fully dressed. At midnight? Thomas wondered why, but only briefly. He quickly went to the elevator and watched the indicator light on the outside. It stopped on the eighth floor. He hit the button and waited impatiently. Alex caught up to him just before he stepped into the car.

"What's going on? Where is Janella?"

"Damned if I know. But I'm sure as hell going to find out. You coming?"

Nodding, Vrooman stepped into the car beside him and Thomas let the doors close and thumbed the eight on the panel. It seemed to take forever, though he knew it had only been a few seconds. When the doors slid open he held them with one hand, poked his head out, glanced up and down the halls in time to see the door to a room just swinging closed. He prayed that was where she'd gone. And for a second he wondered why he was so tense and nervous. It wasn't as if she were in any danger. Why was his neck prickling as if all hell were about to break loose?

Thomas started forward. Vrooman caught his arm.

"You can't just go barging into someone's room in the middle of the night. It might not be the place."

Thomas hesitated. Vrooman had a point. But he still couldn't shake the urgent feeling that had consumed him the minute he'd realized she was gone.

Adrenaline pumped through him, making him nervous and jittery.

"We can listen at the door, see if we hear her voice," Vrooman suggested.

Thomas nodded, and the two men started down the hall.

Janella stood there, and the young man closed the door behind her. She was afraid, she realized as she glanced around the empty hotel suite, seeing no one. Perhaps this was some kind of a trap. Some kind of...

Jack Halloway stepped out of the bedroom, and her blood slowed to a chilled stop in her veins.

"Hello, Janella. Did you come alone?"

She reached behind her for the doorknob, every cell in her body screaming to run for her life. But she froze when another man emerged behind Halloway. His dark hair was sprinkled with gray, and his face had lines she didn't remember. But his eyes were the same, warm and brown, shining now with moisture.

"F-father?"

He smiled and came forward, arms reaching for her, and she flung herself into them. Shaking so violently she could barely breathe, tears flowing now like waterfalls, she clung to his broad back, buried her face in his neck.

He stroked her hair and held her so hard she thought he'd never let go. "Janella? My girl, is this really you?" He pried her away from his chest, clinging to her shoulders, searching her face as tears spilled over his own. "My God, you're beautiful." He pushed her damp hair away from her face, wiped the tears from her cheeks. "Beautiful. My little girl all grown into a beautiful woman," he whispered fiercely, and hugged her tight to him once more.

"Daddy, I don't understand. How..."

"Ah, but it's a long story, child. And we'll have time, so much time now. You're here, right here where I can hold you. That's all that matters now." A sob tore through his chest, and he clung tighter. "You don't know how much I've missed you, baby. How long I've waited for this moment."

Her shoulders quaked with sobs of absolute joy as she held him. And oddly enough, the main thoughts going through her mind were of Thomas. She wished he were here, to share this moment with her. She wanted him right beside her in this room.

She sniffed as her father's hold slackened, and glanced around again, then went stiff as her gaze met Halloway's. His usual grimace had been replaced by a rather dopey smile, and she frowned, instantly suspicious.

"Why is he here?"

The knock on the door prevented anyone from answering. A gun appeared in Halloway's hand. Janella felt her eyes widen as the young man at the door called, "Who is it?"

"Janella, are you in there?"

"Thomas!" Janella started forward, then paused, glancing again at Halloway.

He nodded once and put the gun away. "It's all right. You can let him in."

The young man opened the door.

Relief was evident on Thomas's face as he stepped inside, and Janella ran into his arms, hugging him tightly. But he set her away from him, searching her face, frowning at the tears he saw there. "Are you all right?"

She nodded, smiling as more tears came. "Thomas, look. My father is here. He's here, and..."

Thomas's gaze rose to look beyond her. The two men stared at each other for a moment, and Thomas nodded. But he was already scanning the room, and when his eyes fell on Halloway, they hardened. Alex had crowded in behind him, and Janella saw him close the door.

"Maybe somebody better explain to me what the hell is going on here," Thomas said, his voice dangerously soft. "Halloway, you want to volunteer?"

She saw Alex's hand lift, and in a blur saw it come down again, hard, across the back of Thomas's head. It wasn't until Thomas crumpled to the floor and Alex stood there with the shiny gun pointing at Halloway that she realized what it was he'd been holding.

She dropped to her knees beside Thomas, sensed the suddenly aborted movements of the others in the room.

"Anyone who moves will die," Alex said in a calm, level tone. "Mr. Halloway, if you would kindly drop your firearm to the floor and kick it toward me, I'd be grateful." He leveled his weapon at the man as he spoke, making the polite request into a command.

Halloway's gaze swept the room, and apparently he found no alternative. He removed the gun with two fingers and let it thud to the floor.

Janella bent over Thomas, her fingers finding the cut on the back of his head as she cradled it. She stroked his face and whispered his name, begging him to wake up. If he died...

Alex had herded her father, Halloway and the younger man, whose name she still didn't know, into a small group at the center of the room. He held the gun on them, not looking away, and ordered Janella to get up and join them there.

She stared at the man she'd thought of as a friend and shook her head, ignoring his instructions. "Why, Alex? Why are you doing this? I don't understand..."

"You don't have to understand," he said, his voice flat and emotionless.

"He's a hit man, Janella."

She blinked in surprise at Halloway's voice as he gently answered her question. She knew what the term meant from the movies she and Thomas had watched together.

"He works for your mother."

She shook her head fiercely, staring in disbelief at Alex, trying to follow what she was being told, but not having much success. Alex glanced down at the gun lying near his feet and frowned in concentration. The weapon rose on its own, coming to rest in his free hand. As he tucked it into the waistband of his trousers, Janella finally understood. Alex Vrooman was one of them, one of her own people.

"So you've managed to track me down at last, Vrooman," her father said, sadness and regret tingeing every word. "I knew my wife had sent one of her henchmen to find me, but I had no way of knowing who. Been in hiding ever since I came here."

"You think I don't know that?" Alex seemed so elated, as if he'd finally reached a long-term goal.

"Matalin, I wouldn't have used Janella to flush you out if there'd been any other way."

Matalin nodded in understanding, but Janella didn't understand any of this.

"So, you've won, then," Matalin said tiredly. "I'll surrender to you. You have my word. But you have to let my daughter go. She's not a part of this."

Vrooman nodded grimly. Thomas stirred in Janella's arms, and she saw his eyes open. She ran her palm over his face, knew he was awake now, saw him close his eyes again and lie still, and knew he wanted Vrooman to believe he was still unconscious.

"I would never harm Janella," Vrooman said. "I want nothing but happiness for her. It's the way her mother would want it. Besides, her only crime is defection, and executing her for that would likely stir revolt among the people."

"Not to mention that Shira would have you killed the instant she learned you'd hurt her daughter," Matalin said softly, glancing at Janella. "She doesn't take well to being defied, does she, Vrooman? No matter the reasons, I appreciate your leaving Janella out of this."

"No reason to involve her any further. It's you I was sent for. But you're mistaken if you think I'm here to bring you back."

He pointed the weapon right at Matalin, and Janella cried out. "Stop! Put it down—what are you doing?"

Thomas squeezed her hand in warning.

"My orders are to eliminate you, Matalin. You're an escaped prisoner. You'll be an example to others who think of fleeing our justice." One hand worked the action of the gun. "Your body will be put on display when I return with it."

"Shira knows you've found me, then? She must be celebrating my death already."

"Shira trusts me implicitly, fool," Vrooman growled. "I was sent here years ago with her instructions. She required no reports on my progress, only my word that I'd return with your body. I'd begun to despair of ever finding you, until I was notified that Janella had fled the planet. I knew you'd come out of hiding if word got out that your daughter was here. And so you did."

Vrooman's finger slid over the trigger. Thomas surged to his feet and charged Alex just as the gun went off with an earsplitting roar.

Janella screamed. Halloway shoved her father to the floor at the same instant the gun went off.

Thomas hit Alex hard, like a rampaging bull, and they both slammed into a wall. They struggled, grappling for the gun. Then Alex got one hand free and plowed his fist into Thomas's face. Thomas staggered backward a few steps.

It all happened in a matter of seconds. The young man had managed to get to the door, and flung it open, fleeing the room. The door stood wide, and Janella's father stood at her side, urging her with his eyes to run, pushing her bodily with his hands.

In slow motion she saw Alex raise the gun and point it at Thomas. She saw his finger closing on the trigger, and she screamed, launching herself between them.

The weapon spat fire. Janella stood shocked into motionlessness by the red heat that seared her chest.

She blinked as the room seemed to go silent around her, like a great empty cave. There was a rushing sound in her ears, accompanied by her echoing heartbeat, thudding louder and slower with each second that passed.

She was vaguely aware of her father attacking Alex like an enraged bull, of the gun sounding again as they struggled, of Alex slumping to the floor, his eyes going vacant.

Her knees were melting. Thomas was speaking as he caught her in his arms, his face contorted in agony. She met his eyes as he sank to the floor, holding her, and she saw the blood on his hand when he moved it away from her chest.

She forced her lips to move, forced the words to form, and tried to shout them aloud, even though she couldn't hear them herself. She prayed she could make Thomas hear them, though, before it was too late.

"I . . . love . . . you," she mouthed again and again, and as her eyes fell closed and her grip on reality slipped away, she whispered, "my husband."

Chapter 13

Thomas sipped bitter coffee from a foam cup in the emergency room of the tiny hospital. Matalin sat slumped in a hard-backed vinyl chair, looking shell-shocked and saying nothing. He stared, dazed, at the closed door to the treatment room where Janella had just been taken. Nurses and PAs rushed in and out, but Thomas had yet to see anyone with MD printed on a name tag. And he was just about sick of waiting.

"Duffy, are you listening to a word of this?" Jack Halloway stopped his restless pacing and fixed Thomas with a worried gaze.

"Yeah, I hear you. You guys were the ones protecting them all along. I was an idiot, refused to cooperate with you, and thanks to that my wife is lying in there bleeding from a gunshot wound to the chest. That's the gist of it, isn't it?"

Halloway blew an impatient sigh and shook his head. "I should have told you up-front. But I wasn't sure who Janella was or what she wanted here, and I couldn't risk it. No one outside my agency knows about them, Thomas. And that's the way we want to keep it. They'd never have a minute's peace here if it became public knowledge. And we knew Matalin was a possible target. He told us a long time ago there would probably be someone sent after him. For all I knew, Janella could have been it."

Thomas didn't care. He'd misjudged Halloway, misjudged Vrooman, screwed up royally, and Janella was paying the price.

"This organization Vrooman claimed to represent is nothing more than a group of diehard UFO watchers. None of them has a clue there are aliens living right here among us."

Thomas nodded as if he were listening. He wasn't, though. He'd taken to watching that damned door, just as Matalin was doing.

"To us, they're refugees fleeing a hostile government. We take care of them just as we would anyone seeking political asylum. We've even tried to establish diplomatic relations with their planet, but the bastards up there want no part of it."

Thomas crushed the cup in his hand. "Where the hell are the doctors in this place?" He strode to the door, shoved it open and stomped through, leaving Halloway hanging in midsentence.

A nurse hurried to block his path, but he pushed her aside with no gentleness intended.

"Sir, you can't—"

"I'm a doctor, dammit. Apparently the only one on the premises at the moment." He snatched the chart from the stainless-steel tray and scanned the notes there. Her vitals were weak, and a glance at the digital dial told him her blood pressure was falling, gradually but steadily. "Where the hell are her X rays?"

The nurse seemed flustered, but not willing to argue. She pointed to the wall where the dark sheets were mounted, and Thomas went to them, looked at the story they told, and felt his heart plummet.

The door opened, and when he turned it was to see an elderly man in a white coat. His gaze darted to the name tag and he sighed in relief.

"Finally." He extended a hand. "I'm glad you're here, Dr. Kopelson. Looks like she's bleeding internally. That bullet's lodged tight against the heart, and time is the enemy. She needs surgery, STAT. You'd better go scrub and get these people busy prepping her. I—"

The man held up a hand and Thomas's words died away at the grim expression. "I'm not a surgeon, son. Chief of staff and a plain old GP, but not a cutter."

Swallowing hard, Thomas searched the man's face. "So where's the surgeon?"

"Not here, I'm afraid. Dr. Tanner is on call. He's on his way."

"How long?"

Kopelson lowered his eyes. "An hour. Too long, I'm afraid."

Thomas pushed both hands through his hair, chin falling to his chest. He swore under his breath. "This isn't happening. Dammit to hell, this isn't happening."

"You a surgeon, son?"

Thomas's head came up fast, his eyes meeting Kopelson's worried ones. "Not practicing. It's been months—"

"She's not going to make it an hour, Dr. Duffy. If you try, she might have a chance."

"Dammit, she's my *wife!* I can't—"

"There's no one else."

A lump that nearly choked him settled in Thomas's throat. He turned, walked numbly to the table where Janella lay, pale and still. He took her hand in his, felt its unnatural coolness, gazed down at her face. And he knew, right then, that he loved this woman. He had for a while now; he'd only denied it with everything in him. If he lost her, his life would be nothing but a huge, empty hole. He couldn't let her die. He had to try....

He glanced up at the white-haired doctor who stood nearby. "Prep her. Get me the best surgical nurses you've got."

Kopelson nodded and sent a glance toward one of the nurses, who had all of them moving in an instant. "C'mon, I'll show you to the scrub room."

"In a second." Thomas took one last look at Janella, ran his hand over her cool face. There was no iron wall to stand between him and this patient. No way he could be calm and practical and remove himself emotionally. He loved her. She'd become the most important thing in his world, brought him back to life when he'd been no more than a functioning corpse for so long. He couldn't lose her.

Bending over her, he pressed his lips to hers. "It's gonna be all right, baby. I'll take care of you. I swear it."

When he straightened, he saw a nurse blink tears from her eyes. There were a few in his own right now. And his hands were shaking. Dammit, he had to get a grip, had to make this come out right. Janella's life was in his hands.

Turning, he walked quickly back into the waiting room. He knelt in front of Matalin, clasped the man's hands in both of his.

Matalin met his gaze, devastation in his eyes. "Is she—"

"No. But she can't last long the way she is. She needs surgery, and there's no one who can get here fast enough to do it."

Halloway came to stand behind Thomas. "Except you, right Duffy?"

Thomas closed his eyes, nodded once. Halloway swore.

"I need to know if there's been any precedent. Any of your people, Matalin, who've undergone surgery here. Any reactions they might have had to anesthesia—"

"I don't know," Matalin said, sounding as if it were an effort for him to form the words.

"I do."

Thomas straightened, turned to face Halloway. "Tell me then. Anything that might help."

Halloway nodded. "If I'd handled this differently, she might never have been hurt. Dammit, Duffy, you have to know I never wanted to hurt her."

"Look, if anyone mishandled things, it was me. But there's not time for recriminations now. Tell me what you know," Thomas insisted. "Time is of the essence, Jack."

Clearing his throat, Halloway focused, eyes intense as he scanned his mind for the details Thomas needed. "A woman had a C-section two years ago and died on the table. They used a spinal block. Baby's heart stopped, too, but it was revived."

Thomas blinked, fear creeping up on him darker and bigger than any he'd felt in his life.

"Then there was an emergency appendectomy six months ago. Young boy. They used a general anesthesia, and he came through it all right."

Thomas nodded, turned again to Matalin. "I'm asking your permission to operate on her, Matt. I know you don't know me. You've got no reason to trust me, but I swear, I'll do my damnedest to save her."

Matalin looked up, then rose and stood nose to nose with Thomas. "But I do know you, Thomas. You're the young hero my daughter met in the woods such a long time ago. The one who chased off some toothy creature that frightened her, and brought her back to me, safe and sound."

Thomas's head lowered to hide his damn tears from this man. Remembering her then was almost too much to bear.

Matalin lifted his hand and settled it on Thomas's shoulder. "She talked about you all the way home," he said softly. "Told me she'd never marry, no matter how many choices she might be given in the future, because she'd fallen in love that night. And I have to believe that love survived all the years in between. When she came back here, she came to you. And she stayed with you."

Thomas closed his eyes, remembering with a rush of emotion the words Janella had uttered as she lay bleeding in his arms in that hotel room. Still, he couldn't believe they were true. "There were circumstances—"

"I know all about the circumstances of your marriage, young man. Jack filled me in. I also know what I saw in her eyes when you came into that room tonight. If my daughter loves you—and make no mistake, Thomas, she does love you—then you've already earned my trust."

Hell, the guy was going to have Thomas sobbing too hard to think straight if he kept it up. "Thanks for that," he managed, but his voice had gone coarse and gravelly.

"I'll ask you only one question," Matalin went on. "Do *you* love *her?*"

Thomas stared into those deep black eyes, eyes so much like Janella's. "More than I ever imagined possible."

Matalin smiled weakly and nodded. "At home, they'd have just let her die. No heroes like you there, my boy." His eyes narrowed. "Do you have any idea how beautiful it is, what you do?" He shook his head. "No, I don't suppose you do. It's taken for granted here, isn't it? No matter the injury or illness, your people know that somewhere there's a doctor who will do his utmost, give his all, to save them. How lucky they are to have you among them, Thomas."

Thomas felt new tears well up in his eyes.

"And how lucky I am," Matalin added, "to have you as my son."

Son. God, no one had called him that since his father had died. Hell, he couldn't let Matalin down, not now. The older man gripped Thomas in a surprisingly strong embrace, and Thomas automatically hugged him in return.

When Matalin released Thomas, Halloway slapped his shoulder. "I'll go find that chief of staff guy and see if I can help him get whatever clearance you need to operate here. You get busy. Get your butt in gear and save your wife."

Thomas nodded. "I'll do my damnedest."

Sweat coated Thomas's forehead, no matter how often the nurse beside him wiped it away. But his hands were steady. He was amazed that they were. Maybe they understood how important this was. He'd probably shake like a leaf later, but not now. Not with Janella's life in his tenuous grip.

The bullet lay nestled against the heart, perhaps nicking the muscle. He had to remove it without a single slip.

"Let's be ready," Thomas said. "Watch for bleeders." The nurses scrambled to obey. Thomas carefully got a grip on the small, misshapen hunk of lead with the forceps. A nurse wiped his brow again, but he felt the sweat stinging his eyes. He glanced at the assistant, who stood across from him. "Ready?"

The man nodded.

He heard the door to the OR swing open and close again, but was too focused just now to pay attention. Thomas pulled the bullet away, and another tool was slapped into his hand. He used it like a fast gun from the Old West, repairing the damage. It seemed they all held their breath as they watched to see if the bleeding started again. It didn't, and after a moment there was a collective sigh.

"By God, that was the nicest piece of work I've seen in years."

Thomas glanced up, saw a stranger in scrubs and a surgical mask, with smiling eyes.

"Mark Tanner," he said. "And from the looks of things, I'd say this young lady was fortunate I couldn't get here any sooner. I don't know if I could have pulled that off. Congratulations, Doctor."

Thomas was rapidly going limp now that the crisis had passed. "Thanks," he croaked.

"You wouldn't like me to close for you or anything, would you?"

The man's eyes were still smiling, and Thomas nodded gratefully.

"Glad to. You go somewhere and sit before you fall down. If I had to perform a surgery like that on my wife, I'd be ready for a month in the mental ward."

Thomas glanced back at Janella, then faced the surgeon. "Take care of her," he said, and then he stumbled through the doors. Leaning back against the wall, he tore the mask from his face and dragged in several shuddering breaths. Someone ran toward him, waving smelling salts under his nose. Someone else shoved a wheelchair up beside him and somehow knocked him into it. Probably with a feather, he thought later. He peeled the bloody gloves from his hands, leaned his head back in the chair, closed his eyes and prayed.

And as he did, he realized that he'd never feel the same way about medicine again. Not if he lived to be a hundred. Not if he saw ten million patients between now and then. The iron wall had melted like butter, and even its remains had evaporated, leaving no trace that it had ever been there.

For the first time in a long time, he felt a little giddy at his talent for healing. Like the way he'd felt the first time he'd played nursemaid to a little bird with a broken wing. The elation that had enveloped him as he'd watched the tiny animal take flight again filled him now. He knew instinctively that Janella was going to be all right. And no matter what else might happen between them, he'd pulled her through, saved her life.

It was as if a light inside him had been extinguished for a very long time. Now it was glowing again, with blinding brilliance. Thank God he'd had the skill to do what he had. Thank God he was here for her. He was thrilled to be a doctor again. And he knew that every day, with every patient he saw from now on, he'd let himself feel that joy.

Janella opened her eyes to see sunlight streaming through the white slats that covered a window. She was in a bed, covered with a stiff white sheet. There were tubes in her arms that led to a plastic bag filled with liquid, high on a pole beside her. There were colored wires running from her chest to a tiny TV screen with funny white lines spiking across it.

And Thomas was standing there, holding her wrist in his hand and gazing intently at his watch. She pulled her wrist through his grip until he held her hand instead, and she turned hers to lace fingers with him.

His gaze found hers, and he smiled. "Sleeping Beauty, I guess my kiss finally woke you."

"You kissed me?"

"Once every fifteen minutes for the past several hours. I guess it would have worked faster if I'd been a prince, but there were none available, so..."

"And I wasn't awake to enjoy it," she said softly, pretending to joke, but feeling real regret at the thought.

He bent over her, brushed his fingers through her hair. "Hey, don't worry. There are plenty more waiting for you."

His tone was light, but his eyes more serious.

"Are there, Thomas?"

He nodded. "If you want them, Janella. I'd like very much to wake you with a kiss every morning for the rest of your life and kiss you to sleep every night. Would that be okay with you?"

She blinked in shock, wondering if he was asking what she hoped he was asking. She tried to sit up, and pain split her chest down the middle. She cried out, and his hands eased her back to the pillows.

"Easy, honey. Don't try to move so much. You're gonna have to be still for a while."

It was difficult to be still when her heart's desire seemed to be on the line, right this minute. And when there were so many questions whirling in her mind. "My father?"

"Matt's fine."

"Matt?" She'd never heard anyone call her father "Matt" before, but she thought he might like it.

"I sent a nurse to let him know you were coming around. Alex is dead. Halloway..." He shook his head. "Believe it or not, Halloway turned out to be one of the good guys."

She closed her eyes and sighed. "Then it's over."

"Oh, no, it isn't, Princess. Not by a long shot."

She frowned at him, about to ask him what he was saying, but she stopped when her father came into the room, all the tension fleeing his face when he saw her. He rushed forward, took her hands in his and kissed the backs of them.

"I'd like to hug your breath away, my girl, but your doctor says I have to be gentle."

"I'm so glad to see you," she told him, tears flooding her eyes the second she saw him.

"Me, too."

Thomas cleared his throat, drawing both gazes. "Actually, Matt, you're just in time. I want to do this right, this time."

Janella tilted her head, confused. Her father sent Thomas a wink. "Go right ahead, my boy. Ask away."

Thomas grinned. "Didn't know you were a mind reader."

"I'm not. Just a good guesser. So spit it out."

"What are you two talking about?" Janella asked, feeling she was missing something important.

"I would like to formally ask your permission to marry your daughter, sir."

Matalin grinned. Janella shook her head. "But we're *already* married." She bit her lip. "I mean, technically—"

"Yeah, well, I don't want to be married *technically.*" Thomas glanced at Matalin. Matalin nodded, stepped away from the bed and waved an arm toward it.

Thomas came to the bedside, took Janella's hand in his, and gazed into her eyes. To her utter shock, his own were slightly damp, and his hand was shaking just a little.

"Thomas?"

"Since I came back from the South Pacific I've been a walking dead man, Janella. Or I was until I found you. You brought me back to life again, and if I lose you, it'll be an empty life." He bent closer, kissed her mouth gently, but she could feel the hunger he fought to hold in check.

"I want to marry you all over again. And not because of Halloway or Immigration or what the neighbors might say. I want you to be my wife . . . because I *love* you. I knew that when I almost lost you, and I don't ever want to feel that way again. I need you in my life, Janella."

She smiled. "Do you mean to tell me I had to be shot before you realized it?"

Thomas blinked as if in shock. "Well . . . I—"

"I have been in love with you since we first met, when I was just a little girl. And you, Thomas Duffy, have loved me all that time, too. I've been going crazy wondering how to make you see it, and after all of this, I refuse to give you an answer until you admit it."

"I admit it," he said, looking a bit uncertain.

"That won't do. Don't you realize how I pined for you all those years? And then I come back to you, only to have you tell me you had no intention of ever loving any woman. You owe me for that, Thomas." She crossed her arms—carefully—over her chest and waited.

Thomas frowned, then shrugged. "I dreamed about you after you left. Did you know that? It was the first time in my life I'd ever felt that way for a girl. And the last."

She nodded, watching him. "Go on."

He smiled wickedly at her. "And despite my determination to remain a bachelor, you've been driving me crazy ever since you came back. I think of you my every waking moment, dream of you every night, crave you when you're away from me, lust after you every time you draw a breath, and—"

"All right," she said softly, lifting a finger to his lips to stop the flow of words.

"All right what?"

"All right, I'll marry you. For real this time. I like your tradition of the father of the bride walking her down the aisle to give her over to her husband. Can we do that?"

Thomas nodded, then turned to her father. "You're gonna love Sumac, Matt."

"I hope so," he replied. "Because I intend to make it my home." He gripped the door. "Now, I'll go and get a bite to eat and leave you alone for a while."

He left, and Thomas bent to whisper in Janella's ear, "I've got a suspicion he and Eugenia might just hit it off."

"You have a conniving mind, Thomas."

"Mmm-hmm. And right now it's conniving creative ways I might be able to make love to you without hurting you."

She lifted her eyebrows. "I heal fast, Thomas. And I have no desire to wait very long."

They both laughed, but Thomas's face sobered, and he ran a hand over her cheek, cupped her nape, caressed it with his fingertips. "I can't believe the way I feel about you, Janella. I can't believe how much I love you, or that I'm lucky enough to have you love me back. But it's real, isn't it? It's real. You're mine."

"I've always been yours, Thomas. You're just slow to catch on." She drew him down to her, and he kissed deeply, his mouth hot and demanding against hers. Janella reveled in it. And marveled at it. She'd crossed worlds to find this love, and she would never, never let it go.

* * * * *

Silhouette celebrates motherhood in May with...

Debbie Macomber
Jill Marie Landis
Gina Ferris Wilkins

in

Three Mothers & a Cradle

Join three award-winning authors in this beautiful collection you'll treasure forever. The same antique, hand-crafted cradle connects these three heartwarming romances, which celebrate the joys and excitement of motherhood. Makes the perfect gift for yourself or a loved one!

A special celebration of love,

Only from ▼ Silhouette®

—where passion lives.

MD95

Take 4 bestselling love stories FREE

Plus get a FREE surprise gift!

Special Limited-time Offer

Mail to Silhouette Reader Service™

> 3010 Walden Avenue
> P.O. Box 1867
> Buffalo, N.Y. 14269-1867

YES! Please send me 4 free Silhouette Intimate Moments® novels and my free surprise gift. Then send me 6 brand-new novels every month, which I will receive months before they appear in bookstores. Bill me at the low price of $2.89 each plus 25¢ delivery and applicable sales tax, if any.* That's the complete price and a savings of over 10% off the cover prices—quite a bargain! I understand that accepting the books and gift places me under no obligation ever to buy any books. I can always return a shipment and cancel at any time. Even if I never buy another book from Silhouette, the 4 free books and the surprise gift are mine to keep forever.

245 BPA ANRR

Name	(PLEASE PRINT)	
Address	Apt. No.	
City	State	Zip

This offer is limited to one order per household and not valid to present Silhouette Intimate Moments® subscribers. *Terms and prices are subject to change without notice. Sales tax applicable in N.Y.

UMOM-9295   ©1990 Harlequin Enterprises Limited

And now for something completely different...

SPELLBOUND
ROMANCE

In April, look for
ERRANT ANGEL (D #924)
by Justine Davis

Man in Crisis: Dalton MacKay knew all about grief. It consumed him...until a troubled teen and a well-intentioned teacher barged into Dalton's very private life.

Wayward Angel: Evangeline Law was no ordinary woman—or educator. She was a messenger of hope in a seemingly hopeless case. And her penchant for getting too involved reached the boiling point with sexy Dalton....

**Get touched by an angel
in Justine Davis's ERRANT ANGEL,
available this April,
only from**

SILHOUETTE®
Desire

SPELL8

"Evelyn Vaughn is a momentous storyteller..." —*The Talisman*

Evelyn Vaughn's

The series began with WAITING FOR THE WOLF MOON, SS#8, then continued in BURNING TIMES, SS#39. Now prepare to enter Evelyn Vaughn's "The Circle" once again in May 1995 with BENEATH THE SURFACE, SS#52.

Mary Deveraux knew something was terribly wrong in the Louisiana bayou she called home. She felt the evil as fiercely as she felt her passion for Guy Poitiers—her childhood friend...lover...and next target of the Grim Reaper....

The Circle—Four friends, four magical gifts, four loves to last eternally. Don't miss any of their stories, available only in—

EVCIRC1

Experience the dark side of love in...

In April, enjoy this Silhouette Shadows title:

SS #51 SOMETHING BEAUTIFUL
by Marilyn Tracy

Jillian Stewart's daughter, Allie, was growing
unnaturally attached to an imaginary friend. And
Jillian had become inexplicably drawn to loner
Steven Sayers. But Steven knew firsthand that the
friend Allie called "Something Beautiful" was truly
something wicked that had come for them all....

Experience the power of passion, with the edge of danger in Silhouette Shadows

Available in April at a store near you.

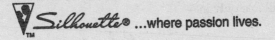

…where passion lives.

SS495

THE MACKADE BROTHERS

the exciting new series by
New York Times bestselling author

Nora Roberts

The MacKade Brothers—looking for trouble,
and always finding it. Now they're on a collision
course with love. And it all begins with

THE RETURN OF RAFE MACKADE
(Intimate Moments #631, April 1995)

The whole town was buzzing. Rafe MacKade
was back in Antietam, and that meant only one
thing—there was bound to be trouble....

Be on the lookout for the next book in the
series, **THE PRIDE OF JARED MACKADE—
Silhouette Special Edition's 1000th Book!**
It's an extraspecial event not to be missed,
coming your way in December 1995!

THE MACKADE BROTHERS—these sexy, trouble-
loving men will be heading out to you in alter-
nate books from Silhouette Intimate Moments
and Silhouette Special Edition.
Watch out for them!

NRTITLE

SILHOUETTE... Where Passion Lives

Don't miss these Silhouette favorites by some of our most
distinguished authors! And now, you can receive a discount by
ordering two or more titles!

SD#05844	THE HAND OF AN ANGEL by BJ James	$2.99 ☐
SD#05873	WHAT ARE FRIENDS FOR?	$2.99 U.S. ☐
	by Naomi Horton	$3.50 CAN. ☐
SD#05880	MEGAN'S MIRACLE	$2.99 U.S. ☐
	by Karen Leabo	$3.50 CAN. ☐
IM#07524	ONCE UPON A WEDDING	
	by Paula Detmer Riggs	$3.50 ☐
IM#07542	FINALLY A FATHER by Marilyn Pappano	$3.50 ☐
IM#07556	BANISHED by Lee Magner	$3.50 ☐
SSE#09805	TRUE BLUE HEARTS	
	by Curtiss Ann Matlock	$3.39 ☐
SSE#09825	WORTH WAITING FOR by Bay Matthews	$3.50 ☐
SSE#09866	HE'S MY SOLDIER BOY by Lisa Jackson	$3.50 ☐
SR#08948	MORE THAN YOU KNOW	
	by Phyllis Halldorson	$2.75 ☐
SR#08949	MARRIAGE IN A SUITCASE	
	by Kasey Michaels	$2.75 ☐
SR#19003	THE BACHELOR CURE by Pepper Adams	$2.75 ☐

(limited quantities available on certain titles)

AMOUNT	$_____
DEDUCT: 10% DISCOUNT FOR 2+ BOOKS	$_____
POSTAGE & HANDLING	$_____
($1.00 for one book, 50¢ for each additional)	
APPLICABLE TAXES*	$_____
TOTAL PAYABLE	$_____
(check or money order—please do not send cash)	

To order, complete this form and send it, along with a check or money order
for the total above, payable to Silhouette Books, to: **In the U.S.:** 3010 Walden
Avenue, P.O. Box 9077, Buffalo, NY 14269-9077; **In Canada:** P.O. Box 636,
Fort Erie, Ontario, L2A 5X3.

Name:_____

Address:_____ City:_____

State/Prov.:_____ Zip/Postal Code:_____

*New York residents remit applicable sales taxes.
 Canadian residents remit applicable GST and provincial taxes.   SBACK-MM

Silhouette®